BUSTED

Also by Phil Bildner

Playing the Field

Phil Bildner

Simon & Schuster Books for Young Readers

New York · London · Toronto · Sydney

SIMON & SCHUSTER BOOKS FOR YOUNG READERS
An imprint of Simon & Schuster Children's Publishing Division
1230 Avenue of the Americas, New York, New York 10020
SIMON & SCHUSTER BOOKS FOR YOUNG READERS is a trademark of
Simon & Schuster, Inc.
Book design by Alicia Mikles
The text for this book is set in Janson Text.
Manufactured in the United States of America
2 4 6 8 10 9 7 5 3 1
Library of Congress Cataloging-in-Publication Data
Bildner, Phil.
Busted / Phil Bildner.—1st ed.
p. cm.
Summary: Interweaves stories of students at a high school with a "zero-tolerance" policy as
they get caught doing things they are pretty sure are wrong, from drinking and having sex
during a senior ski trip, to organizing a gambling ring, to bullying freshmen, to honor stu-
dents behaving dishonorably.
ISBN-13: 978-1-4169-2424-1
ISBN-10: 1-4169-2424-8
[1. Conduct of life—Fiction. 2. High schools—Fiction. 3. Schools—Fiction.] · I. Title.
PZ7 B4923Bus 2007
[Fic]—dc22
2006037305

This one is for my friend Christian,
the bravest kid I know. Hang in there, buddy.
It gets better. I promise.

BUSTED

Zero Tolerance

The Assembly

"I'M TELLIN' YA, THERE'S NO WAY they'll bed-check every room," Casey said.

"You know Bratten will," Todd replied, sizing up the chaperones seated on the auditorium stage. "So will Curtis. They have to. To keep credibility."

"Dude, no way. They're only checking a few rooms. Everyone we've spoken to said that's how they did it last year."

"You know they'll check ours."

"T, to be honest with you, I don't care what they do." Casey leaned into his best friend sitting beside him. "No way am I spending a night in the same hotel as Nikki and not getting some. Not happenin', dude."

"Heard that." Todd tapped Casey's hand, fingers-to-fingers then knuckles-to-knuckles. "No way am I spending a night in the same hotel as Joanne and coming home with my virginity!"

"Dude, you're gonna be a man in a couple days. The cherry's getting popped."

"You know it."

"I still can't believe Jo's partaking in the late-night *festivities*. About time she decided to give it up. What made her finally come around?"

"What do you think?" Todd smiled cockily. "She finds me irresistible."

But of the two, Casey—and not Todd—was the cocky one. At Coldwater Creek High School (or any high school, for that matter), it comes with the territory when you're a third-year starter on varsity basketball *and* baseball, and you have the Hollister looks to back it up. And when you also happen to be a member of the National Honor Society and French Honor Society all four years of high school, you *know* you're the complete package.

Casey was the leader of their duo. Not that Todd was a follower. It was just the way things had been between them ever since they had become friends at the start of middle school. Casey was always the one lighting the fuse of their plans, schemes, and adventures. Not that Todd ever really minded or resisted. Like in ninth grade when they used to take Casey's dad's Jaguar out for late-night spins. And all those weekday afternoons when Todd would be babysitting his sisters and Casey would show up with a beer ball and the basketball team.

"Your bro's definitely coming through for us?" Todd asked.

"No doubt." Casey checked the time on his cell and tapped the screen. "In fact, I bet Señor Jose Cuervo's already waiting for us under my pillow."

"God, I hate tequila."

"Dude, we're gonna get so hammered."

"After what happened last year, could you imagine if they busted us tequila drunk?"

"Not happenin'."

"What do you think they'd do?" Todd asked.

"Not happenin'," Casey repeated.

Todd never minded or resisted Casey's living on the edge. But Todd still was the more cautious member of the tandem. He always allowed himself—at least initially—to look at the risks and dangers involved. Though it rarely stopped him.

"What's the worst that's gonna happen?" Casey asked, whenever he sensed (and he always could) even the least bit of hedging in Todd. "You get in trouble. You get punished. Your mom's disappointed in your behavior, your choices, and your decision making. Big deal. In the grand scheme of things, it's nothing. Nothing but a great story you'll be bragging about to your fraternity brothers and all your boys for the rest of your life. Dude, by the time you're telling your grandkids about it, it'll be an exaggerated legend of biblical proportions."

Once things started to roll, Todd's hesitance always disappeared, and he grabbed the reins and liked to push the envelope even further than Casey.

"But say it was all four of us," Todd pressed, "and we still had the bottle, and—"

"Dude, give it a rest."

"What if Drew and Brad and—"

"Dude, that's why those boys aren't partying with us. All of us together would be inviting trouble."

"What about if Shane and Dex—"

Casey reached over and palmed Todd's mouth. "You're not gonna stop till I answer, are you?"

Todd shook his head and freed his grin from Casey's hand.

"Didn't think so." Casey sighed. "If we got busted, Zig would shoot first and ask questions later. And after what went down last year, it wouldn't be pretty. That's what this assembly is really about. So here's my solution. You ready? We don't get busted. End of story." They tapped hands again, fingers-to-fingers then knuckles-to-knuckles.

"This is gonna be off the hook."

"No doubt."

"You're leaving here at seven thirty tomorrow morning. That doesn't mean get here at seven thirty. It takes time to load the buses, take attendance, and make sure everything is set. If you want to be at the mountain and out on the slopes by noon, you need to be here on time."

Principal Danzig peered out at the sea of disinterested faces and half-shook his head. They had heard all this before from him. Several times, in fact. And now they were hearing it yet again. They *needed* to hear it again. That was why he had called this final assembly—to remove all doubt. No matter what, he was not going to shoulder *any* of the blame or responsibility when things didn't go perfectly—and things never went perfectly—on the senior ski trip, the annual rite of passage for students at Coldwater Creek High School. Each year someone always had to step out of line, or fail to follow instructions, or tempt fate and test his edicts—as if that were somehow part of the rite of passage too.

"If you're one of those who has problems with alarm clocks, or if you're one of those with time issues who likes to cut things close, trust me, tomorrow's not the day to push your luck. You show up here at seven thirty, seven forty, thinking they're holding the buses for you, think again."

"Do you think they should come back with us straight from dinner or wait till after curfew?" Joanne asked.

"Do we really have to plan this now?" Nikki rolled her eyes. "We're hooking up with our boyfriends, Jo, we're not planning a hostile takeover."

"Haven't you listened to a word Zig's been saying?"

"Girl, I stopped listening to this crap three meetings ago."

Joanne tapped the page stapled to the front of Nikki's trip folder. "'In order for your senior trip to run smoothly,'" she read, "'it is imperative to adhere to all timetables, plans, schedules, and arrangements.'"

"Jo, we're getting some after-hours action." Nikki swatted her best friend with the folder. "It's not like we need to purchase tickets in advance."

But if tickets were available in advance, Joanne was certainly the type of person who would buy them. Among their circle of friends, she was the responsible and organized one. Everything always needed to be in order. And since tomorrow night was not only going to be a special night with her friends, but also *her* night, more than any other time, things needed to be perfect.

"Do we have the alcohol yet?" Joanne asked.

"Casey's brother's taking care of it." Nikki nodded. "You know that."

"That means we're drinking tequila."

"Which means we're having a blast."

"Do you think he knows to get salt and lemon?"

Nikki rolled her eyes again. "You're worrying way too much about things we don't need to be worrying about."

"If we're drinking tequila, I need to worry. Two shots of that stuff, and I'm done. And without salt and lemon, forget it! So I'm getting them, just in case."

"I think you're taking your planning a little too far."

Joanne had started planning their "Night to Remember" more than a month ago. And while her friends never missed a single opportunity to rib her for mapping out every last detail, she knew they appreciated her efforts.

Joanne had coordinated everything, even the room assignments, so that everyone roomed with the people they wanted, and no one felt slighted or left out. And when it was decided that Joanne and Nikki's room would be "Party Central," and that they would be going two to a room instead of four like everyone else, she convinced everyone to help cover the difference in cost.

"I just want everything to go perfectly," Joanne said.

"Everything will, Jo. It's going to be the most memorable night of your life. Just like it should be. But if you're going to be buggin' out like this, you're going to drive everyone crazy."

"I think I'm allowed to bug out a little. It's not every night I sleep with my boyfriend for the first time."

Nikki laughed. "You and Todd have absolutely nothing to worry about except getting caught, and since that's not happening, no worries. Simple as that."

"You think other people are gonna be partying like us?"

"What kind of a question is that? I don't think there's a person in this auditorium who's not!"

"Even after these assemblies? And after what happened last year? If you get busted, you're totally screwed."

"Listen, Jo, I'm partying and gettin' my groove on. You should too. This is your senior ski trip. But if you're gonna be this much of a buzzkill, maybe you should just bring a book instead, or play video games with Shane and Dex."

"I just don't want to get caught."

Nikki shook her head. "I always knew my best friend was a worrier, but now you've turned it into an extreme sport." She waved at the stage. "You're not getting caught. This is all a show. To cover their asses. We're seniors at the Creek. When push comes to shove, they're powerless to stop us."

"Ladies! Keep it down!" Principal Danzig smacked an open hand on the side of the lectern. "We're not leaving here till we get through this, and I need at least twenty more minutes up here. The more you continue to interrupt, the longer this is going to take."

He reached into his trip folder, the identical blue-and-yellow packet issued to each of the students, and pulled out the double-sided page containing the daily itinerary.

"As far as the check-ins go, the teachers will designate the exact time and place once you get to the mountain. There will be *two* check-ins each day. Do not miss *either* of them. Yes, you're free to travel wherever you want at the mountain—any of the trails, the superpipe, the tubing park, the lodge—but make sure you and your ski buddy are at those check-ins."

"Sure thing, Zig!" a student in the back called out.

The auditorium laughed.

Principal Danzig managed a wave and a smile. His job still had its moments. While he hated the frustrations and demands and injustices and expectations and no-win situations—all of which seemed to increase by the day—he still enjoyed the kids. Through it all, that's what kept him going. And it always would.

"Trust me." He placed both hands on the lectern. "I'm going to be neurotic about those check-ins, and I'm allowed to be. This is an etched-in-stone zero tolerance policy. If I start getting phone calls this weekend about missing students, I will not be a happy camper. The only thing I want to hear from these teachers up here is that they saw *all* your pretty faces *all* four times. Is that clear?"

"Crystal!" another voice called out.

The auditorium laughed again.

Principal Danzig laughed too and then turned to the row of faculty members. "Is there anything else I need to cover before I talk about the hotel? Ms. Curtis, anything you can think of?"

He intentionally singled her out first since all the

students knew her. She was head of the social studies department, and every student had her at one time either for Global Studies or American History. And a large number also had taken her legal studies elective as juniors and seniors.

"I don't think so," she replied.

"Mr. Lansing, anything else come to mind?" Principal Danzig worked his way down the line. "Ms. Nixon? Mr. Bratten?"

Mr. Bratten's name was greeted by a series of giggles, and Principal Danzig instantly fired a glare in their direction. He knew exactly why the teacher's name had elicited such a response. Everyone at Coldwater Creek High School knew why.

On last year's senior ski trip, when the six students had gotten caught smoking pot at the rest stop by the state trooper, it was Mr. Bratten who had been forced to wait with them until *each* of their parents had driven the ninety miles to pick them up. No student had been permitted to leave until *every* parent had arrived. That was the only way all six had been able to avoid being arrested. So, while the rest of the group had gone ahead to the mountain, Mr. Bratten had been stuck at the rest stop for nearly ten hours. And, since none of the students would own up to their actions, it was Mr. Bratten—knowing how stoned they all were—who wouldn't let them even get a sip of water.

"If you're not talking," he had said, "you're not drinking, putting your head down, or even going to the bathroom until your parent is here."

His actions earned him the nickname the Sheriff from the students.

And while Principal Danzig had found Mr. Bratten's conduct more than a little harsh, in light of the circumstances, it was understandable. Since he had saved half a dozen of his students from going to jail and, more than likely, appearing on national newswires, it was difficult for Principal Danzig to be anything but understanding and grateful.

"The series of events that unfolded on that trip was easily the most unpleasant I've ever been forced to encounter," Mr. Bratten vented to him on several occasions afterward. "Professionally and personally, it was the worst experience of my career. Never again will I place myself in such a position."

After the ski trip incident, Mr. Bratten had refused to participate in any off-site school-sanctioned activities, and Principal Danzig had been in no position to object. And when some parents and faculty had rallied to cancel this year's trip, Mr. Bratten had been the loudest voice of all.

But that was where Principal Danzig drew his line. That was not how he ran *his* school. It went against all of his principles and philosophies. A high school that punished one group of students for the sins of another group did not work, and he would not stand for it. Not from anyone. Not even from one of his best and most reliable teachers.

Which was why he had called Mr. Bratten into his office six weeks earlier and had made him the offer.

"I'd like you to be the lead chaperone for the senior trip again."

"Is this some kind of joke?" Mr. Bratten had replied. "Are you trying to be funny? I don't find this—"

"You'll be paid an extra four thousand dollars in cash for the weekend." Principal Danzig's words had stunned Mr. Bratten. And his next sentence had absolutely floored him. "This exchange doesn't leave this office."

"Could anyone get in trouble for this?" Mr. Bratten had asked.

"As you know, we have a Friends of the Roaring Rapids account," Principal Danzig had replied without answering the teacher's question. "When the parents' association does their fund-raising, that's where the money gets deposited. After last year's fiasco, they knew to earmark extra monies for this year's trip."

"Can I get back to you in a day or two?"

"No," Principal Danzig had replied flatly. "I'll need your answer now. And if you accept and the other teachers learn of it, you will forfeit the stipend."

"Let's make it an even five thousand," Mr. Bratten had boldly countered.

Principal Danzig had stared him down. It was common knowledge in the community that this administrator's tactics sometimes stretched the limits of propriety, but he never allowed anyone to test or challenge those limits.

"This isn't a negotiation, Mr. Bratten."

"You need me. Otherwise, you wouldn't be asking me."

"That's correct," Principal Danzig had replied sharply. "I need you for this. There's no other teacher I can depend on, but *I'll* dictate the terms. Four thousand. Yes or no?"

Mr. Bratten had accepted.

Which was why he was sitting on the auditorium stage right now.

And at this moment, as Principal Danzig locked eyes with him, they both knew that if anything were to happen, if all hell were to break loose another time, Mr. Bratten was going to be the one to have to deal. Not Ms. Curtis. Or Ms. Nixon. Or Mr. Lansing. For the most part, the others were merely warm bodies along for the ride, and one or two probably needed as much supervision as some of the students.

"Imagine if we got busted."

"Don't even go there." Dex removed his earpieces hidden underneath his CCHS-embroidered baseball cap. "Not even as a joke."

"You wanna talk zero tolerance?" Shane chuckled. "My 'rents would disown me."

"Ditto."

"Nah, your folks would be all right."

"Not about something like this." Dex slid his iPod into his pocket. "And can we not have this conversation?"

"I'm telling you, D, your 'rents would be okay."

"Shane, I'm serious. Can we not play this game?"

"They'd be a lot more understanding than mine."
Shane patted his friend's leg. "My mom would go
religion on me."

Dex glared. "Shane, stop. Our parents aren't
finding out, we're not risking it, and this conversation is over."

"So you don't want to anymore?"

"What are you talking about?" Dex made a face.
"Are you kidding?"

"You just said you didn't want to risk it."

"Right, I don't want to risk it, but I still *want*."
Dex smiled.

"Just making sure."

"Yeah, but you do need to chill right now."

A smack hit the back of Shane's head. He ducked
away and turned.

"What are you two girls plotting?" Casey
smacked at him again and then draped his arms
around his two friends sitting in the row in front of
him. "You girls gonna party with the big kids, or is
this gonna be another all-night video-game fest?"

"Haven't decided yet." Dex swatted at Casey with
his cap.

"Well, make up your minds."

"We're rooming with you, Case." Shane lifted the

arm from his shoulder. "I promise, you'll know before Brad or Drew or anyone."

"We'll decide when we get there," Dex added. "We're on the bubble 'cause we're afraid of the Sheriff."

"Well, whatever I can do to alleviate those fears and persuade you to partake in the festivities, you let me know. It's our Night to Remember."

"Last, but not least," Principal Danzig said, "the hotel. Tomorrow evening."

He waited for total silence before continuing.

"When you get there, which will be around six thirty or seven o' clock, it's going to take a good half hour to get everyone checked in and assigned to their rooms. Dinner's going to be from eight to nine. After that, the evening's yours."

As expected, his last sentence was greeted with soft laughter, murmurs, and chatter. He waited for it to completely subside before going on.

"After dinner, you're going to have two hours to yourselves at the hotel. You need to use your heads. You're in a public place. Despite what you may think, you're not the only ones staying there. You need to respect the hotel, and you need to respect the other guests. Keep the noise levels down, especially the later it gets. At eleven fifteen, the teachers will be going room to room for check-in. At that time, everyone will be in his or her own room, and that's where you'll stay. Period."

His last sentence was greeted with more murmurs and chatter. He waited again for silence. And when he had it, he paused before starting back up.

"I'm not going to get into last year again, but I will say this: Don't call this bluff. Hear my words. Trust me, this isn't an 'I dare you.' This is a zero tolerance policy. Zero tolerance. Violate the rules, your parents will be contacted. Violate the rules, you will be called before the school board and ordered to publicly explain your conduct. Violate the rules, you will be suspended. Violate the rules, you will not be permitted to attend the senior prom. Violate the rules, you will not be permitted to march at graduation. Zero tolerance."

Principal Danzig closed his folder and stepped in front of the lectern.

"And I'm going to say one more thing." He pointed at the crowd. "For this one night, sexual conduct of any kind will not be tolerated. Yes, I am preaching abstinence. I know you're teenagers in a hotel, and I know many of you are past the age of consent, but tomorrow night you're going to have to exhibit a little self-control. No, we haven't set up cameras in your rooms, but I am warning you, keep your pants on. For this one night, there's no gray area. And yes, you can view this as a threat if you want to. Trust me, zero tolerance."

The Hotel

"WE ALL SET?" Casey stood by the door, tapping his foot in mock impatience.

"Doing one last sweep," Todd replied, going from bed to desk to end table to bathroom.

"You nervous?" Shane asked.

"Nope. Just making sure I got all our goodies."

"T, you're definitely nervous." Dex paused the video game and put down his controller. "We've had to stop three times in the last minute."

"Last chance." Todd stood in front of Shane and Dex, who sat on the foot of the bed. "You sure you don't want to join us? Throw on some sweats. We'll wait."

"No, we're good," Shane replied.

"Well, when you light up in here" —Casey placed his hand on the knob—"take the nine-volt out of the smoke detector."

"What makes you think we're blazin'?" Dex asked.

"It's all you two ever do. Blaze and play Halo or Halo 2 or Halo 6 or whatever," Todd said as he headed for the door. "Which way is the Sheriff's room?" he asked Casey.

"All the way down on the left."

"Then we go right."

"Brilliant, brainiac." Casey patted Todd's head. "But I'm tellin' ya, after the day Bratten had, we could be partying outside his door, and it *still* wouldn't matter. After what he went through last year, and what he didn't have to go through this year, he was creaming in his pants! Cancel his Viagra 'script 'cause he won't be needing that anymore."

After skiing and before heading for the hotel, Mr. Bratten had made a point of boarding all six buses and thanking everyone for not only arriving on time in the morning but also making the check-ins. At dinner, he had beamed like a proud parent.

"What do you think?" Todd turned back toward Shane and Dex. "Should Señor Cuervo go in my cargoes or my hoodie?" He placed the bottle of tequila, wrapped in a pillowcase, in a side pocket of his pants and then in the pouch pocket of his sweatshirt.

"T, it don't matter," Casey answered first.

"Don't be so cocky, Case," Dex warned. He restarted the game.

"That's not being cocky." Casey grabbed a pillow from the top of the open closet and flung it at Dex. "That's saying you're screwed either way if someone sees you."

Dex ducked without looking away from the television. "It was less obvious in your pants."

"But I'll have to limp." Todd placed the bottle back into his cargoes.

"Dude, you're not limping 'cause of the bottle," Casey said, laughing. "You're limping 'cause you already got a hard-on thinking about Jo."

"No doubt!" Todd and Casey tapped hands like they always did. "I'm finally scorin' tonight!"

Casey glanced at Shane and Dex as he reached for the door again. "Boys, don't do anything we wouldn't do."

"That goes for you, too," Shane replied.

"You ready, T?" Casey tapped Todd's chest.

"Ready."

"Cell phones are off?"

"Check."

"Condoms?"

Todd patted his pocket. "Double check."

"We'll be back later, boys."

"Much later."

"I still can't believe we have to use bottle caps for shot glasses," Joanne said, looking at the mouthwash and moisturizer caps lined up on top of the television.

"It's not like we have a choice," Todd said.

"Well, if I'd been allowed—"

"Everyone's got a lemon and salt?" Casey cut her off.

"Of course we do." Nikki passed out the caps of tequila. "Thanks to Jo."

Joanne gave her the finger. "I need a breather after this one, or I'm going to be a mess."

"Girl, you already are a—"

"Don't finish that thought!" Joanne pointed the same middle digit at Nikki.

"It sure is going to be interesting on the slopes tomorrow." Todd smiled. "Half-pipe hangovers!"

"Speak for yourself, T." Casey laughed. "Some of us can handle our liquor."

"You can handle your liquor?" Nikki messed her

boyfriend's hair. "I can't remember the last time you didn't puke after doing shots."

"What do you think the teachers are doing now?" Joanne asked.

"The ones who aren't sleeping?" Todd draped his arm around Joanne and smiled as he always did when he had any alcohol in him. "They're doing the same thing we are!"

"For sure!" Casey reached for Todd's free hand, and tapped it. "That's why they got their rooms three floors up. Out of sight, out of mind. After how perfect today was, they don't wanna have to start busting anyone."

"Bratten deserves mad props." Nikki raised her cap. "He put together a kickin' day."

"I'll second that." Joanne tapped her cap and then began distributing the lemon slices.

"But before we drink this one, I have a real toast." Casey placed his arm around Nikki and huddled all his friends in close. "You know I'm buzzed 'cause I'm about to get all corny."

Nikki kissed his cheek. "You're always corny."

He waited for Joanne to finish shaking the salt onto each of their hands. "Today was absolutely off the hook, tonight is off the hook, and tomorrow's gonna be off the hook." He looked at each of his friends. "Check out where we are! This is our senior ski trip. It's the middle of the night, and we're chillin' and partyin' just like we planned. In a few months, we're gonna be graduates from Coldwater Creek—"

"You're rambling, Case." Nikki interrupted him with another kiss. "Some of us want to drink."

"You guys rock," he continued. "Here's to the rest of our senior year. And here's to our friendship."

"But we're missing Shane and Dex," Todd said.

"And everyone else, for that matter," Joanne added.

"Shane and Dex had their chance," Casey replied. "And as far as everyone else goes, they're here in spirit. You know they're partying just as hard in Liz's room, and I can only imagine what Brad and Drew got going. Did you see the size of the bottle Drew brought?"

"We couldn't all be together," Casey continued. "We knew that coming in. Way too risky. So on three, friendship!"

"One, two, three, friendship!"

As if the routine had been rehearsed numerous times before (which it had), they each licked the salt pinched between their thumb and index finger, downed the shot, and sucked on the slice of lemon.

"Okay, I have something else," Joanne announced.

"You do?" Nikki said. "I didn't see anything in your BlackBerry."

Joanne swirled her middle finger and pointed it at Nikki again. "Be a bitch and you don't get any." She picked up her travel bag and dropped it onto the bed, nudging at Casey and Nikki, who were already lying down and making out. "You two are gonna need to come up for air. Party time!" She reached into her makeup kit and pulled out a joint.

"You rock!" Todd hugged her so hard they fell on top of Casey and Nikki.

"I wouldn't have expected this from you," Casey added. "Maybe Nikki, but not you. Well done!"

"Nice," Nikki cheered. "Who's got the light?"

Silence.

"No!" She sat up quickly. "No one's got a lighter?"

"Good planning, Jo," Casey said, smirking.

"There has to be matches in here." Joanne reached for the end table. "Check the drawers."

"Not a chance." Nikki pointed to the THANK YOU FOR NOT SMOKING sign above the mirror.

"This sucks!" Joanne smacked the bed. "I've rolled the most beautiful J in the world, and all we can do is look at it."

"I guess we'll have to think of other things to do." Todd rolled on top of her and began kissing her neck.

"I'll get a light." Casey stood.

"Where you gonna get a light?" Nikki asked.

"Our room."

"No, you're not." Nikki swatted him. "That's the stupidest thing I've ever heard. You're gonna risk getting caught for a lighter?"

"It's not a risk. It's almost one o'clock. They're not policing the halls anymore."

"You're drunk." Joanne slid from under Todd and sat up.

"Easy, Jo." Casey slid his feet into his flip-flops. "Not everyone falls out after three shots. I'll be back in less than a minute."

"You want company?" Todd offered.

Casey waved him off. "Nah. It's all good. I'll see if I can drag Shane and Dex back. Once they hear we're smokin', that might motivate 'em."

"Text them first," Todd said. "You'll freak them out just showing up. You know how paranoid Shane can get when he's stoned."

"Don't I know it! That's why I won't be texting him." Casey popped a piece of gum into his mouth and kissed Nikki's neck.

She pulled away. "I'm going on record and saying you shouldn't go."

"I second that," Joanne added, "and that's my joint, and I *really* want to burn."

Casey stopped at the door. "I tell you what, ladies. Close your eyes and start counting. By the time you get to a hundred, you'll be drunk *and* stoned."

"Casey!"

He couldn't even pretend not to hear the voice behind him. His gut reaction told him to run, but he couldn't. He was in the middle of the corridor. No-man's-land.

He quickened his pace anyway.

"Casey!"

It was futile. The voice closed too fast. Casey stopped, but he didn't dare turn around. He chewed hard on his gum.

"You mind explaining what the hell you're doing out of your room?" Ms. Curtis asked angrily.

Casey lowered his head before pivoting around.

"Why are you out of your room, Casey?"

He glanced up, but didn't reply.

"Did you not listen to a single word Principal Danzig said yesterday? Did you really think he was kidding?"

Casey still did not speak, but as he looked at Ms. Curtis, he could see her discomfort and unease. This was the last place she wanted to be too.

Did my friends hear? Can she smell my breath?

"I'm getting Mr. Bratten," Ms. Curtis growled. She pulled out her cell.

"Is that absolutely necessary?"

"Is what absolutely necessary?"

"I mean, do you have to call him?" Casey exhaled a deep breath. "Can't we just pretend that you never saw me and . . ."

"What are you saying, Casey?"

Casey shut his mouth and looked away. Even he knew when to stop.

"I'm getting him right now." Ms. Curtis punched in the pre-programmed number and waited for Mr. Bratten to answer. "He's going to be just as thrilled about this as I am. Nice work, Casey. Way to the ruin the trip."

Casey knew better than to answer her back. In fact, he knew not to say anything further at all. Ms.

Curtis had taught him that in *her* legal studies class.

"If you ever get caught doing something you're not supposed to be doing, say nothing," she had lectured on more than one occasion. "Wait for your parents or a lawyer or a responsible adult, because no matter what they're telling you and no matter how nicely they're treating you, anything you say can and will be held against you."

Casey leaned against the wall and coughed into his hand. At least the gum was camouflaging the tequila, he thought.

"He'll be out here in a minute." Ms. Curtis snapped her cell phone closed and hooked it back to her belt. "You have a hell of a lot of explaining to do, Casey, considering he'll smell you from down the hall."

Yes, they had heard. They had heard everything.

The room door had barely clicked closed, Joanne had counted only to seven, and the conversation hadn't even started up again when they all heard Ms. Curtis. "Casey!"

They instantly leaped into cover-up mode: Caps, lemons, and salt packets brushed behind the television; food, clothing, and wrappers swept from the beds; tequila bottle buried in the garbage.

Joanne grabbed the clicker, hopped onto the bed, and pretended to watch the muted television, while Todd dove under the far bed and draped the bedspread over him.

"Should I hide in the bathroom?" he whispered.

"Shut up!" Joanne ordered. "Can you see anything?" she asked Nikki, who was looking through the peephole.

She didn't respond.

"Can you hear anything?" Joanne pressed.

"Nothing." Nikki turned around. "This is so fucked up. He never should have gone."

"I can't stay under here like this," Todd said.

"Stay there!" Joanne dropped her leg off the bed and kicked at him. "And shut up!"

Todd shielded his head and giggled nervously. At the moment, he hated that alcohol always made him smile and laugh. "Jo, don't be yelling on me."

"Don't be yelling? Your best friend is getting screwed."

"I can't exactly do anything about it."

"We're next! What do we do?"

"Jo," Nikki's voice rose to above a whisper, "you need to chill."

"I agree." Todd crawled out from under the bed. "You think I should run for it?"

"I have to text Casey." Nikki spoke to the door.

"His phone's off." Todd sat up. "What a buzzkill."

"This is the definition of a buzzkill." Nikki turned around.

"Should we text Shane and Dex?" Joanne placed a hand on Todd's shoulder.

"And say what?" he asked.

"This is so not how things were supposed to happen." Joanne shook. "Tonight of all nights!"

"Jo, chill!" Nikki sat on the bed beside her. "Any chance Curtis and Casey will come back here?"

"Only if she saw him leave from here," Todd replied.

"She didn't. When I shut the door, she wasn't there." Nikki turned on her cell. "I'm trying Casey."

"Wait a minute, Nikki." Joanne's voice broke. "We're panicking. We can't panic. We can't—"

"It's pointless to call him," Todd interrupted. "His phone's off."

"Then if his phone's off, he won't answer!" Nikki snarled. "But I'm pretty sure it's on. I had my hands in his pockets."

"You work fast." Todd smiled.

"Go to hell. If he can speak, he will."

"If you're gonna call or text anyone," Joanne said, "you should try Shane and Dex. Warn them."

"That's assuming they're not already in there," Nikki said. "If we call, and they're in there, we've just turned ourselves in."

"This is so fucked up." Joanne echoed Nikki's words from moments before.

Todd stood up. "Well, I can't stay here."

"Where are you going?" Joanne asked.

"I can't stay here, and the longer I am here . . . I have to try to get back there before they do."

Nikki shook her head. "Todd, face it. Bratten and Curtis are already waiting in your room."

"You can't know that."

"Of course they are."

"I don't think so." Todd was now standing against the far wall. "I can't stay here. The longer I'm here—"

"What if they're still down the hall?" Joanne asked.

"What if they're not?" he snapped.

"They'll see you leaving here."

"What choice do I have?" Todd grabbed a pillow off the floor and pounded it with his fist. "Jo, I'm sorry, but I need to bolt." He kissed Joanne on his way to the door. "My only chance is to get back to the room before they do."

"Todd, think about us," Joanne pleaded.

"I am!"

"You're not! You're being selfish!"

"No!" Todd tried not to yell. "I'm thinking about Casey, and I'm thinking about Shane and Dex, and I'm also thinking of you two."

"You're only thinking about yourself. If they see—"

"What if they find me here, Jo? Bratten's no dummy. He'd bring Casey to Nikki in a heartbeat. Then we're all screwed!"

"Well, if you're doing your thing," Nikki said, opening her phone, "I'm doing mine."

"This is so fucked up."

"How stupid can you be?" Mr. Bratten pointed his finger in Casey's face. "Do you realize what you've done?"

Casey didn't respond. He leaned against the wall, intentionally pressing on his back pocket so that his cell phone powered up.

"Quite the situation we have here, isn't it?" Mr. Bratten swatted Casey's shoulder with a trip packet.

Casey's thoughts remained with his friends.

They have to know something's wrong. I've been gone ten minutes. Where is Todd? Is he still with them?

"Look at the position you've put me in," Mr. Bratten continued. "Look at the position you've put *everyone* in. Did you not hear a word Principal Danzig said?"

"He's not going to say anything." Ms. Curtis frowned. "He hasn't said a word the entire time."

"He said, 'zero tolerance,' Casey, and he meant it." Mr. Bratten opened the folder and smacked the page. "It doesn't matter who you are."

Casey rubbed the back of his neck.

Shane and Dex smoked. The room has to reek. How can I warn them? Have the others called ahead?

"You taught him well, didn't you?" Mr. Bratten turned to Ms. Curtis.

"Too well."

"At least he listened to someone." Mr. Bratten paced the hall and then stopped in front of Casey again. "Let me tell you something, Casey. Your silence isn't helping matters. I know you're not the only one involved in this, whatever *this* may be. When we get back to your room . . ."

Mr. Bratten continued to speak, but for the moment, Casey did not hear. It was time to stall. The longer the delay, the better the chance that Todd could get back to the room before they did.

Casey grabbed the back of his neck a little tighter. They *had* to have heard, he told himself. Ms. Curtis had stopped him only a few doors down.

"And let me tell you something else, Casey." Mr. Bratten's words began to register again. "If we have to sit up all night in order to get to the bottom of this, we will. I'll give you one last—"

The vibrating hum of Casey's phone. An incoming text.

Casey shifted his look from teacher to teacher.

"You going to get that?" Ms. Curtis asked.

Mr. Bratten reached out. "Maybe you'd like me to?"

Casey pulled back.

"You're digging yourself quite a hole, Casey." Mr. Bratten shook his head. "And just so you know, if that was a text, and I'm pretty sure it was, your friends are even bigger idiots than you are. You don't think we're going to find out who sent it?"

The phone stopped.

"Let's go, Casey." Ms. Curtis started down the corridor.

"Yes, let's go." Mr. Bratten motioned for Casey to walk ahead of him. "Now."

Casey started slowly.

"Pick up the pace," Ms. Curtis snapped instantly. "We're not playing games with you."

"Ms. Curtis," Mr. Bratten said, "Casey's going to do whatever Casey wants to do. But it's going to be a completely different story when I have his father on the phone at two in the morning telling him he *needs* to come pick up his son."

They rounded the corner and approached the room.

"Lemme have your key," Mr. Bratten ordered.

Casey pulled the card key from his pocket, but didn't hand it over. He wanted to open the door. He wanted to walk in first.

Please be there, Todd. Please don't let the bud be out.

"I said, give me your key."

But Casey stepped up to the lock anyway. He could hear the video game and see the flickering television under the door.

"Mr. Bratten." Casey finally spoke. "Whatever you . . ." He stopped himself.

"You want to say something, Casey?" Mr. Bratten glared.

Casey only frowned.

"Afraid of what we're about to find on the other side of that door?"

Casey drew a long breath and slowly lowered the key into the slot, intentionally placing it in upside down. He nosily rattled the knob.

"Not a time to be playing games," Ms. Curtis snapped again.

Casey placed it in again, this time with the magnetic strip reversed. He rattled the knob.

"Open the damn door, Casey!"

Casey flipped the key and slid it in correctly.

The lock clicked.

Mr. Bratten pushed open the door.

Neither Dex nor Shane heard the jiggling knob.

Nor did they hear the opening door.

Dex was on the floor, kneeling at the foot of the bed. He was shirtless, his embroidered CCHS baseball cap on backward. His head was between Shane's legs, and Shane lay on the end of the bed, with his Umbros and boxers around his shins.

Shane cried loud, uncontrolled sobs. He was panting, almost hyperventilating, curled fetal-like on top of the pillows of the far bed. His head pressed so hard against the wall it hurt, but he didn't care, too overcome by the shame, fear, humiliation, and horror. His eyes were half-closed slivers, his vision blurred and hazed by his tears. He wouldn't dare look in the direction of his friends. He couldn't face them.

Casey felt Mr. Bratten's eyes staring through him, but he didn't look his way. If he had, it would have meant seeing Shane, and at the moment, Casey wasn't sure if he could handle that. He was having a hard enough time just listening to him in such a state.

Besides, Casey didn't need to look at Mr. Bratten in order to know what he would see. He knew Mr. Bratten hadn't moved, still seated at the foot of the bed with his hands clasped behind his neck and his forearms like a vise around his head.

For certain, Mr. Bratten's face still held that same expression. The one that screamed, *I was wrong*. The one that said that after last year, after he had thought he had seen everything, and that nothing involving students could *ever* catch him by surprise again, this had. Even Mr. Bratten hadn't envisioned this scenario. Even he couldn't have played this one out in advance. That's why his expression contained that hint of a smirk and a tinge of a disgusted smile. Almost as if he had somehow known he would eventually find himself in this position, the exact position he swore he would never allow himself to be caught in again.

So as Casey sat on the floor against the closet, hands dangling limply between bent knees, he fixed his eyes on Ms. Curtis. She sat on the sofa along the window, clutching the armrest and trembling. No, shaking. Refusing to even so much as offer a glance in his general vicinity.

This was her fault, Casey told himself. If only she had allowed him to disappear down the hallway. If only she had made like the unfortunate encounter had never happened. Out of sight, out of mind. Ms. Curtis was the one who could've avoided this entire situation. She could've been asleep right now. But no. Instead, she found herself awake in this nightmare. She stared helplessly at Mr. Bratten, who was sitting in the very spot where Dex had been.

Dex. And Shane. The image dominated Casey's head. Like a DVD frozen on a frame.

Suddenly, the ringing of a phone jolted his mind. His eyes darted and landed on Dex.

The phone rang a second time.

Dex looked up. They locked eyes.

But Casey didn't recognize his friend's look. It was one he had never seen before. Still, Casey knew every last word it was saying.

Dex grabbed the brim of his cap with both hands and covered his ears.

I'm sorry, Casey. Don't hate me, man. Help me. Please. What should I do? What should I do, Casey?

The phone rang a third time.

No one was supposed to know. No one was ever going to know.

He and Shane had turned off the music *and* paused the game. And when Shane had accidentally rolled over onto the controller and restarted it, they had stopped in a heartbeat.

The phone rang a fourth time.

This can't be real. This can't be happening.

And moments later when it had happened again, when Shane had inadvertently started the game back up for a second time, they had stopped instantly.

Dex pressed his hands harder against his head.

But when Shane had rolled onto the controller that third time, things had gone further. By that point, the only sounds Dex could hear were the ones of pleasure coming from his friend.

The phone rang a fourth half ring and cut off.

Please be understanding, Case. I'm sorry, man. I'm so sorry.

Dex whimpered.

Everyone was going to know. Everyone was going to find out. Suddenly, the panic and disappointment and fear and *everything* was rising, percolating to the point where he didn't know how much longer he would be able to contain it or if . . .

The sound of a card key.

The turn of the knob.

The creak of the door.

Todd.

"Welcome," Mr. Bratten greeted him with sarcasm. "Please, Todd, come on in."

Todd stood by the door and tried to make sense of the scene. Of his friends, only Casey looked his way.

"Don't just stand there. Join the party." Mr. Bratten walked over and motioned him into the room. "We have quite the situation on our hands. Perhaps you can help us out a little." He sat back down and pointed Todd into the room.

Todd cleared his throat into his hand. His breath *screamed* alcohol. "What's up?" he asked too innocently. He stepped around Casey and sat.

"I want all of you looking at me." Mr. Bratten's

sarcasm disappeared. "Now!" he raised his voice. "Even you, Shane."

Shane didn't react.

"Shane, don't make this any worse than it already is." Mr. Bratten's voice grew much louder. He turned to Todd. "What's up? You want to know what's up? Maybe you should be the one telling me, Todd. Ms. Curtis found Casey in the hall. Any ideas what he may have been doing there?"

Todd turned to Casey.

"Look at me!" Mr. Bratten yelled. "Any guesses as to what we found when Ms. Curtis and I escorted your friend back here?"

Todd turned to his friends again. The tears streamed down Dex's face, and Shane's cries turned to wails. Dex reached back to touch Shane's leg, but Shane recoiled, and the wails grew louder.

"Dammit," Mr. Bratten said. He rested his thumbs beneath his chin and covered his face with his hands.

"Is there some way . . ." Casey started to speak, but stopped himself just as he had in the hallway.

"Is there some way what, Casey?" Mr. Bratten stood up. "I'd love to hear what you have to say about this mess."

Casey didn't respond.

"Didn't think so." Mr. Bratten walked to the sofa and sat down beside Ms. Curtis. "Principal Danzig couldn't have been more clear at that last assembly." His voice rose again. "You knew the rules, and you knew what the consequences would be if you violated those rules"

"Especially after last year," Ms. Curtis added.

Todd shook his head. "Look, I don't know what happened in here, but from the—"

"You're right, Todd." Mr. Bratten cut him off. "You *don't* know what happened in here! You have no idea what happened in here. But in due time, you're going to. And so is everyone else for that matter. Because *I* have no choice. Principal Danzig, parents, the school . . ."

"No!" Shane shrieked. "No!"

Todd lurched. "What the hell happened in—"

"Don't speak!" Mr. Bratten held up a silencing hand. "Do you understand the position you've put me in? Put *us* in?" He was shouting. "This is the absolute worst-case scenario. This wasn't just one rule, this was . . ." He stood up and slammed his fist against the wall.

"No!" Shane cried. "You can't! You can't." He

sobbed the words. "This is . . . this is my life."

"Mr. Bratten, please," Dex pleaded. "Don't do—"

"Don't do what?" Mr. Bratten pounded the wall again. "There's too many of you! And I know it doesn't stop with just you four!"

"No!" Shane screamed.

"Mr. Bratten, there has to be another way." Casey stood up and stepped forward.

"Oh, so now you have something to say?" Mr. Bratten stepped to Casey.

"I don't think you're being reasonable."

"You don't think *I'm* being reasonable?" Mr. Bratten moved to within inches of his face. "You reek of alcohol, this room smells like a drug den, we all walk in on these two over here, and you're talking to me about being reasonable?"

"All I'm saying is—"

"What are you saying, Casey? Tell me." But Mr. Bratten didn't let him answer. "In a few minutes, that phone call to Principal Danzig? I'm not the one placing it. You are. You're waking him up. Not me. You're telling him what happened. You're telling him that *each* of your parents needs to come pick you up because there's no way in hell I'm letting *any* of you get back on that bus."

Casey exhaled. "Mr. Bratten, I don't think you need to make things worse than they already are."

"Really?" He looked to Ms. Curtis and then back to Casey. "*I* shouldn't make things worse than they already are? Casey, I didn't create this situation. You did. You made this mess. Blame yourself. Not me. Take some fucking responsibility."

"Fine, Mr. Bratten," Casey replied defiantly. "I'll blame myself. I'll take some *fucking* responsibility. But that doesn't mean you have to go and—"

"You just don't get it." Mr. Bratten cut him off again. "You really have no idea what you've done here."

"Yes, I do."

"No, you don't, Casey." Mr. Bratten lowered his voice. "Because if you did, you'd realize I have no options."

"Mr. Bratten, there are always options. There has to be another way."

"No, Casey. There isn't. There is no gray area. That's the problem when you play with zero tolerance."

The Ejection Game

1.

"THIS IS BRUTAL," I said to my boy Travis sitting next to me.

"Wicks, you complainin' already? Class hasn't even started."

"Why are we here? Why do we subject ourselves to this?"

"Yo, you gonna be whinin' like this all period?"

I flipped him off.

"I'll take that as a yes," he replied.

I rapped the face of my watch against the desk. Time stood still in Ms. Nixon's classroom. Sure my after-lunch-food-coma-malaise slammed the brakes on any weekday, but the clock stopping in here was something more. Had to be. Especially Fridays. Fridays it was magnified by the powers of many. When the weekend was a mere three periods away, time simply halted. I swear, sometimes the hands on that clock above the door jumped backward.

"Why do we torture ourselves like this?" I went on. "It's not like we've understood a word she's said all week."

"Neither has she." Travis laughed softly.

"This is pointless. Let's bounce, bro. We can—"

The angry smack of an open hand cut our conversation.

"If you know everything," Ms. Nixon screamed, "you get up here and teach the class!"

All heads turned.

"Are you . . . are you talking to me?" Brittney asked. She pointed to herself.

"Who do you think I'm talking to?"

"You are talking to me."

"Of course I'm talking to you!" Ms. Nixon smacked the desk again. "It's not like there's anyone sitting behind you in the *back* row, Britt-ney. Oh wait, maybe there is. Do you have an imaginary friend with you today, Britt-ney?"

"Did I . . . did I do something wrong?"

"'Did I do something wrong?'" Ms. Nixon sassed. "You disrupted my class, Britt-ney. If you think you know so much . . ."

"Ms. Nixon, I dropped my pen." Brittney waved her ballpoint.

"Don't you dare interrupt me while I'm teaching!" She flung the cap of the dry-erase marker in Brittney's direction. "If you're such a know-it-all, you do this. You do my job. You get up here and teach this class!"

Brittney didn't flinch. She didn't when the cap had flown by. She didn't now.

"I'll give you a choice, Britt-ney." Ms. Nixon charged down the aisle. "Either get up there and teach this class, or get the hell outta here!" She hovered above Brittney like a menacing movie drill-sergeant over an insubordinate officer.

"Ms. Nixon, I think you're being unreasonable. I think—"

"Get out! Get the hell outta here! Go to the office! How dare you talk back to me! I don't want to see your face in here until I discuss this matter with *both* your parents."

2.

INTRODUCING MS. VICTORIA NIXON. My math teacher. Typical public high school math teacher:

limited educational skills. Negligible social skills. Nonexistent classroom management abilities.

But with Ms. Nixon, there's also something else. Something more that makes her stand out. And that is, Ms. Nixon is no longer a nice person.

Crisp.

I call her a Crisp. My word for burned-out teachers. Teachers who have overstayed their welcome in the world of secondary education. Or any level of education, for that matter. Maybe at some point Ms. Nixon possessed that idealistic-teacher passion, hunger, and drive. But no more. A Crisp is a hanger-on with no business standing in front of "the leaders of tomorrow." A Crisp goes through the motions. In the door with the first period bell. Out the door with the last.

In my *Webster's*, Ms. Nixon's picture is next to "Crisp". See also "burned", "done", or "toast".

It almost goes without saying that Ms. Nixon is set in her ways. She can only see things her way. Often, that's the wrong way. Often, it's always been the wrong way.

That hasn't mattered. Until now.

It matters now because "her way or no way" is doing damage. Ms. Nixon's lost patience. If someone doesn't understand, someone is denigrated.

In Ms. Nixon's world, in math class, "someone" equals "student."

Frustration is now the key trait that defines her. A frustration of knowing what is, what has been, and what never will be again. The frustration manifests itself in ugly ways. It has made her mean.

The student gets blamed. Then the system gets blamed. Then society gets blamed. Everyone gets blamed.

Except Ms. Nixon. Ms. Nixon is never to blame. Ms. Nixon points fingers.

She has favorite targets, too. Some deserving. Of course some are deserving. This is high school.

But then there are the others. The easy prey. The students you feel bad for. The students you pity. The students who shouldn't have to be subjected to the wrath of an evil and tyrannical Crisp. The students whose only transgressions are that they don't understand.

That's what has triggered the backlash.

The students have struck back. There's only so much you can put up with. And students know how to fight back. They take it to the next level. Push buttons. And they know *exactly* which buttons to push.

Do it without remorse too. No feelings of "cut the old bag some slack." Not in here. She deserves it.

But now, the striking back—the backlash—has led to a response. An escalation in the hostilities. Full-fledged fighting. War.

And in an act of desperation, in an act of a *Crisp*, Ms. Nixon has opted to exhaust and unload the ultimate weapon in her arsenal. She throws students out. Instantly. Everyone's at risk. Anyone is fair game.

The enemy has turned irrational.

Quite the atmosphere we have here in sixth-period math.

3.

"THE LADY'S TYPE VICIOUS," I whispered to Travis while Brittney gathered her belongings and obeyed the harsh directive.

Travis said nothing.

Unless you wanted to be next, it was best to remain silent during a Ms. Nixon toss-out tirade.

He waited until she restarted teaching (using the word in the loosest sense) before speaking. "Yo, who you think's next?"

"Next what?"

"Next to get tossed?"

"Thrown out?"

"Uh-huh," Travis replied. "Who's Nixon's next victim?"

I smiled.

Who is next?

I surveyed the class. A good crowd for a Friday. Almost thirty students. Usually that many showed up only early in the week. By Friday, the number usually dwindled down closer to twenty.

Who is next?

Typically, three to five students were *asked* to leave. Brittney's "get-out-get-the-hell-outta-here" had taken place on the early side, but that didn't necessarily mean it was a heavy-flow period. There was little rhyme or reason to Ms. Nixon's madness. She didn't go after a female followed by a male. Or target one side of the room and then the other. Her attacks were random. Like that of a terrorist. That's what made them so unsettling and, at this moment, so difficult to predict.

Who is next?

"Prob'ly Lance," I finally answered. "Nixon's always picking at him. Maybe Lisa. Or Kim."

Travis held up a finger. "You only get one."

"You're making up rules?"

"You get one pick; I get one."

"If we don't shut up, it's gonna be one of us."

"Yo, I wouldn't mind gettin' tossed. Liz's already waitin' on me in the student lounge."

"You still think you have a shot with that?" I snickered. "You are seriously delusional, bro."

"I *know* I have a shot."

"She's so playing you, Travs. On the days she's in here, I watch it from a front row seat. She's a senior on the Rapids in Motion dance squad. She's not gonna start hitting it with some soph."

"Yo, I'm tellin' ya. I'm feelin' her, and she's feelin' me. I will tap that." He glanced toward the front of the class. "Come and get me, Ms. Nix," he taunted.

"You wouldn't leave me in here all alone."

"Wicks, I love you like my own, but if you're askin' me to choose between your ugly face and Liz, I'm out."

I paused for a sec. "I know how to get you to stay. Let's make this interesting."

"Make what interesting?"

"This." I tapped the desk. "Right now. Let's make this interesting. A little wager."

"A wager on what?"

"On who gets booted."

Travis grinned. "Yo, I put twenty on me!"

"Nah, you can't bet yourself. And you can't get me thrown either. We both gotta pick someone else. Pick the person. You win. Simple as that."

Travis reached into his jeans for his money.

I pulled out my wallet.

And that's how it all began.

4.

"YOU DON'T KNOW HOW TO DETERMINE the factors of sixty-four?" Ms. Nixon stormed across the front of the room.

Alberto swallowed. "Ms. Nixon, I thought you were—"

"You think you're going to get special treatment from me, just because they moved you ahead a year? Just because you're a freshman in a class with sophomores?"

"Ms. Nixon, I was going—"

"How can they have possibly put you in tenth-grade math? How did you make it through middle school? This is fifth-grade material."

"Well, can you show me?"

"I'll show you." Ms. Nixon reached Alberto's

desk. She grabbed his textbook, flipped to the front, and slammed her hand on the open pages. "Read one of these for a change! You do know how to read, don't you? Or are we still doing Hooked on Phonics?"

"I can read, Ms. Nixon," Alberto answered steadily.

"You could have fooled me. The only skill you've demonstrated in this classroom is the ability to tune me out! You certainly have a handle on that."

"I always pay attention in your class, Ms. Nixon."

"Oh, you do? Then how come you still don't know this? If you paid attention, I wouldn't have to *show* you any of this."

"I always pay attention in your class, Ms. Nixon," Alberto repeated. "Just because I don't understand something doesn't mean—"

"Get out! Get the hell outta here! You're wasting my time and the class's time. This is nonsense. Utter stupidity."

Alberto stared up.

"Did you not understand what I said?" Ms. Nixon barked. "Do I need to draw you a picture?"

Alberto picked up his books and left.

As the door clicked close, Travis placed his open hand on my desk and wiggled his fingers.

I pulled out the ATM-new twenty. "You suck,

bro." I smacked the Andrew Jackson into his palm.

"Easy money," he gloated. "Easy money."

5.

A LITTLE ONE-ON-ONE, *mano-a-mano*, small-scale dueling between friends. The perfect way to pass the time on a Friday afternoon.

I put twenty on a name. Travis put twenty on a name. Pick the person. Win the cash.

Travis did.

We bet again on Monday. And Tuesday.

I swear, the Crisp's class never went so fast.

Of course, we added a couple wrinkles to our little contest. Twenty now bought us each two names, and we waited until the end of class to cash out. If we both won, the class was a wash.

"I want in."

Travis and I spun around and faced the words greeting us before the start of class on Wednesday.

Liz.

Liz Martinez. The supersmart senior. Ms. Nixon's so-called student assistant who earned two community service credits simply by sitting in on the class three times a week. Liz did nothing, except read *Us Weekly* or *CosmoGIRL!*, which she kept strategically placed in her lap. And unlike the rest of us, she could engage in such conduct without fear. She was not a potential target, so long as she did not disturb, so long as she remained silent.

Her only threat was Travis. Because Travis had the hots for her, and he would try anything to engage her. It's pathetic to watch. My boy had no chance, but no matter how many times I tried to tell him, he refused to accept reality.

"I want in," she repeated.

"You can't." I waved her off.

"Why not?"

Didn't have a reason. Didn't need one. My game. My rules.

Travis smirked.

I flipped him off.

"This is between me and Travis," I said. I glanced at Ms. Nixon, safely scribbling equations on the board. "Anyway, you're a teaching assistant. You're not a student."

"That's bullshit." Liz tossed her twenty onto Travis's desk anyway. "I'm in."

"Class already started." I placed the twenty back on her desk.

"Class hasn't started."

"The bell rang three minutes ago."

"The Crisp hasn't turned around." Liz smacked the twenty back onto Travis's desk. "Class *hasn't* started. I'm in."

Travis was way too amused by the exchange, and I wanted to smack *him*.

"I'm also making a rule," Liz added, playing with the zipper on her Rapids in Motion hoodie.

"*What?*"

"I'm also making a rule."

"You can't make a rule. This isn't your game."

"Sure I can. You can't bet on anyone on this side." Liz sliced the room with her hand. "You can only bet on the kids closer to the door. There's more kids on that side, and you're less apt to instigate an ejection."

"Instigate an ejection?" I said.

"It's a good rule."

"She's right." Travis nodded. "It is a good rule."

I stared at Liz. Then glared at Travis.

But they were right. It *was* a good rule.

And just like that, the little one-one-one, *mano-a-mano*, small-scale dueling between Travis and me suddenly transformed into a three-for-all.

6.

OUR THREE-FOR-ALL lasted all of one day.

Four more wanted in on Thursday, and on Friday, there were eight of us.

By then, the contest no longer worked. Couldn't. Not like that. It was chaos. An unorganized mess.

"So much for our little game," Travis said, while Ms. Nixon was going gangsta on two students who had both laid bets.

"What are you talking about?" I answered.

"This sucks."

"I'm surprised at you, Travs. You usually have a good eye for potential."

Travis made a face. "Wicks, you're insane."

"This could be huge."

"Whatever, yo."

"I tell you what, Travs." I placed my hand on his shoulder. "After class, go puppy-dog after Liz. When she blows you off like she has the last three days— even though she's 'feelin' you, and you're gonna 'tap' that—come to my crib."

Travis swatted my hand and flipped me off.

But less than two hours later, we were chillin' in

my basement, playing Madden and formulating the rules of the Ejection Game.

7.

THE FIRST RULE OF THE EJECTION GAME was there were no *official* rules. Only a basic framework.

Initially, we weren't even going to write anything down. Didn't want a paper trail. But after a couple minutes of brainstorming, we realized we needed hard copy.

So we grabbed my math assignment pad. Where else were we going to write it down?

"No one's going to like this," Travis said, as soon as we started putting pen to paper.

"Then they don't have to play," I told him. "All we're trying to do is bring a little unprecedented excitement to room three eighteen. We just wanna make Nixon's class—"

"*We? We're?* You got a pronoun problem, Wicks?"

That's the part that Travis didn't like. He didn't want it to be *our* game. He wanted it to be *my* game.

"This is *your* idea," he said. "I'm here for the video games and moral support."

No worries. I was cool running the show. Just

needed someone who had my back. Because I was gonna be telling people you had to play by the rules, and ignorance was no defense. Didn't want anyone accusing me of changing bylaws and making things up as I went along.

Especially with money changing hands.

If you wanted in, it was gonna cost. Twenty-dollar start-up. The initiation fee. Admission.

But for that twenty, I was giving value. Opportunity *and* entertainment. 'Cause this was for entertainment purposes only.

But entertainment came with a price tag. I didn't have the go-green to bankroll the whole thing. If someone won large the first day, I was done. By having everyone front me twenty, I had my safety net. And the Andrew Jacksons also let me know they were serious. I wasn't the only one with my neck on the chopping block. The Ejection Game was risk. I could have gotten in mad shit for it.

Because of Zig.

Principal Danzig was on the warpath those days. After what went down on the senior ski trip (again), it was common Creek knowledge he was looking for balls to bust. Even the Crisp liked to remind us of that. Usually when she was in the middle of sending someone to his den. The Crisp had been on the senior trip, and while she wanted us to believe she was in the center of the storm, I had it on good source she slept through everything. She didn't even learn anything until the next morning.

Still, with or without ski trip disasters, Principal Danzig had been known to lose his shit when it came to illegal activity at the Creek. Especially when the illegal activity was gambling.

Last year a whole lot of juniors and seniors were placing bets on college and pro football games all season. Turns out, Zig knew about it all along, but he waited until the Friday before Super Bowl before busting the ring wide open.

He went off. But word is, he wished he hadn't because the gig turned out to be Reggie Burks's brainchild. National Honor Society, ticketed-for-a-full-ride-wrestling-scholarship, asset-to-the-community Reggie Burks. And because Zig had made such a stink of things, he had no choice but to go downright medieval on him. Suspended him for two full weeks, followed by three months' detention and a semester's worth of community service. The real kicker—he reported the boy to the IRS. Medieval.

Zig also banned every name in Reggie's bookie

book from all Creek functions, clubs, organizations, and teams for a month.

Still, the Ejection Game was different. This wasn't gambling-gambling. Yeah, it involved betting, but not betting in the usual sense. It was people poker.

Entertainment.

Now, as far as the bets went, the lines were clear and straight:

No me-bets. Couldn't bet yourself.

Couldn't try to get your pick thrown out either. That was playing with marked cards. Not happening. And if I suspected it, I was judge and jury. No discussion.

No bets on the same person two days running. Eventually that person was going to get booted, and I was eventually going to end up on the short end.

All individual bets cost five. Pick an ejectee, and your five paid you ten. You doubled your cash. Could also place an option. Let you put two names under the same five. But in order to collect, both names had to get tossed. Pick both, your five earns you twenty. Pick one, *nada*.

Betting started as soon as I got to school. Windows closed at twelve thirty. Fifteen minutes before class.

Recommended: Place bets early. If there was too much action on one person—and I determined what constituted *too much* action—curbs and ceilings kicked in. The name was no longer in play.

Sound good?

Did to me.

Come Monday, the Ejection Game began.

8.

I COULDN'T WAIT FOR NIXON'S CLASS, though I knew me heading to math with over two bills in fees and bets was the sole reason for the alien feeling. Of course, the number wouldn't be that high every day. This was the initial spike I needed to fund the operation.

All my players nodded or waved as they entered. And as more filed in, a strange energy started to build. Anticipation. Excitement.

Once class began, there was this ongoing trading of nervous glances. Anxious smiles. There was also a level of *attentiveness* that had been MIA all year.

Who was it going to be? Who was going first? Who was winning the inaugural installment of the Ejection Game?

What a juice!

Luck had it that for the first time in recent recollection, there wasn't a single "get-out-get-the-hell-outta-here" during the first twenty minutes of class.

Had the Ejection Game somehow altered the classroom?

Hardly.

A first ejection occurred. Then a second. Followed quickly by a third.

And a fourth.

No, thankfully, the Ejection Game had not disrupted the dynamic and flow in room 318.

But more thankfully, no one won. Not a single person nailed any of the ejectees.

Was this how it was going to be? Had I just discovered the easiest and quickest get-rich scheme ever invented by a tenth-grade math student?

I didn't allow myself to hope up. This had to be an anomaly. A quirk. Things would be different and back to normal tomorrow.

But define "normal."

On Tuesday four more students opted into TEG—

that's what I had tagged it by then and the number of bets doubled. There would be a winner that day. Had to be.

There were two.

I paid out twenty in winnings. Didn't mind at all. I was still way ahead, and payouts were great for business.

The next day I had more new players and even more bets. Even had one rookie put down twenty-five in names. He came up empty.

TEG was blowing up. Fast. Over half the class was now involved, and my assignment pad could no longer cut it. So I started logging action in a black-and-white composition. So much for no paper trail (again), but in case of absolute emergency, all physical evidence remained easy to shred.

I was well aware of the increasing risk, and a growing part of me was thinking about taking the money and running.

"If things don't feel right," I told my players, "I'm closing shop. And you're out your bills. No remedy. No recourse."

But I wasn't closing TEG. This was a blast!

I paid out three new winners on day three. Two of the winners picked the same ejectee. And for the first time, one of my TEG bettors got the heave.

Each day, a new twist. Each class, a new wrinkle.

Yes, I had figured it out. I had figured out the key to surviving Ms. Nixon's tenth-grade math class. I had the formula. I had the equation. I *owned* the solution.

9.

MY NEWFOUND ABILITY to impulse-purchase items for the wardrobe and to download unlimited videos to my iPod hadn't completely clouded my judgment. I recognized the Ejection Game needed toggling. Some fine-tuning.

The composition notebook was no longer cutting it, so I went even more old school. Invested in a grade-school Trapper Keeper. Three-ring binder. Pocket folders. Zipper close. The whole nine. Needed my house in order.

I also needed to limit the number of new admits. I now had almost twenty players on my roll. On a high-interest day, I had two thirds of the class running. I needed to seal. At least until I came up with a way to regulate volume.

I needed to amend the framework, too. In fairness, I gave a heads-up and opted not to impose the alterations until Monday. My clients understood. Nature of the beast.

First, I expanded the consecutive-days betting rule to include Friday–Monday bets. You couldn't bet a person Friday and then bet that same person on Monday. At the same time, I instituted "CAR," the "capping out rule." I was noticing betting patterns, and I didn't want players always placing their money on the same name. Under CAR, a bettor was only allowed to bet the same name seven times. After seven, the bettor permanently capped out.

I had to make the changes. With so many players in the fold, with so many names being played, and with so much money changing hands, I was losing my edge. Couldn't afford to lose my cash cow.

Yeah, it was more work for me, but it was well worth the investment.

I was considering even more changes too, and these additional changes were gonna piss players off. Maybe even send a few away. But this first set of changes was my way of easing into it.

I wanted to completely replace the consecutive-day rule with a rule banning bets on the same person twice in the same week.

I also wanted to create an additional bet that

allowed players to place one ten-dollar "bonus" bet per month. Paid four-to-one, or forty dollars.

Finally, I also wanted to introduce an alternative betting method because I wanted more money up front. Under this new approach a player could place *all* bets for the week before class Monday. This was a tough sell, so for every five bets, the bettor received a sixth one free. Had to offer some kind of incentive. Absences were always an issue in Nixon's class (though substantially less since TEG, I might add), and under my rules, you had to be present to win. It was also far more difficult to predict throwing-out patterns a week ahead of time. Some students might not light their fuse until Tuesday or Wednesday. A bettor who placed their bets on Monday was precluded from capitalizing on the burning.

But all of this was still only in my head. I hadn't decided if I was going this route. It was all still new. Still plenty of time to figure out the finer details.

10.

"YO, YOU'RE SO GONNA get busted," Travis said.

We were back in my basement playing Madden.

"How am I gonna get busted?"

"Wicks, you're takin' bets in the hall, in the lounge and in the cafeteria. People are talkin'."

"What's the worst that can happen?"

Travis pressed PAUSE. "Don't want to find out."

"TEG's the best thing that's ever happened to Nixon's class. Attendance has never been higher."

"Like you can take credit for that?"

"I am the reason."

"Who's gonna care?"

I restarted the game. "Kids haven't paid this much attention to that Crisp in years."

"Wicks, you're missing the point. You can't be serious, trying to defend yourself like this."

"I won't have to, bro."

"If Zig catches wind of this, he'll go ballistic. He'll make—"

"This is so different," I cut him off. I knew where Travis was going. "Reggie was a full-fledged bookie."

"Wicks, Reggie was the golden boy since middle school. But not anymore. He's totally lost his shit. He can't wrestle, and he might not even graduate."

"I'm no golden boy, Travs."

"No, but you get decent grades and you're only a soph. You got a lot to lose."

"What's your point?"

Travis shook his head. "My point is . . . just don't push things too far. Reggie's life's a mess. Suspended. The Feds."

"Travs, I'm not running a ring! TEG is innocent in-class fun."

"Innocent? Yo, if it's so innocent, do it *dinero*-less. See if anyone plays."

"We're having fun in math. No one's getting hurt. What's the big deal?"

"All I'm sayin' is be careful."

I stood up. "Travis, this is a shared learning experience."

"Oh, shit. Here it comes."

I pretended to roll up my sleeves. "Look at the exposure to mathematical principles I'm presenting. I'm providing what Nixon no longer can. Basic accounting. Probability." I counted fingers. "Investment equations. Portfolio management."

"Portfolio management?"

I was rolling. "Administration. Introduction to business models. Organizational skills. Entrepreneurship."

"Yo, you've given this way too much mind."

"Travs, you know I'm right."

"But who's gonna care? You can spew every educational and mathematical buzzword known to student-kind. But Zig still won't give a shit."

"We'll see, bro."

"No, I hope we won't."

11.

"YOU NEED TO STOP!"

I recognized the voice, but I didn't bother turning around. The words coming from down the hall couldn't be directed at me.

"Wicks!" the voice said. "You need to stop!"

I was wrong. I turned to find Reggie Burks, growling down at me with no regard for personal space.

"You think you're so smart, don't you?" He poked a finger into my chest.

I swallowed hard.

Reggie Burks knew my name? Knew I existed? What could Reggie Burks possibly want with me?

"Why are you pilfering my game?"

I had no idea what he was talking about, but I was too scared to speak. And of course, there wasn't a single other person in the hallway. This was bad.

"You think you can just waltz on in and replace me, Wicks?"

"Reggie, I don't . . . I don't know what you're talking about."

"You know *exactly* what I'm talking about. You think I don't know what's going on in Nixon's class?"

How does he know?

I swallowed even harder. "We're—we're just playing a game."

"Game over!" Reggie grabbed my arm. "You got balls pulling a stunt like this. You got a big pair for a soph."

I didn't know whether to agree or disagree.

"What should I . . . What do you want?"

"Right under Zig? Right under me?" He still had my arm. "Who do you think you are, taking my game?"

"What game?"

"That's *my* game you're playing."

Reggie shoved me into the lockers. Not hard. But hard enough.

"The Ejection Game?" I asked.

"Yeah, your little eject game or TEG game or whatever you're calling it."

"We're just having fun. I made it up . . . 'cause— 'cause Nixon's class is mad brutal."

"You didn't make it up."

"Yeah, me and—" I stopped myself.

"What? You didn't think I'd find out?"

A bead of sweat rolled off my brow and down my cheek. Reggie's smirk told me he saw it. He pressed me harder against the locker. The handle dug deeper into the bottom of my back.

"Do you know who my girl is?" Reggie asked.

I said nothing. Now I *really* didn't like the direction he was headed in.

"I chill with Elizabeth." Reggie was nodding. "Yeah, Elizabeth. Same Elizabeth your boy gives the hard sell to."

"Listen, Reggie—"

"Man, that little shit'll say anything trying to get a piece. Like he's got a prayer in hell."

"Listen, Reggie—"

"No, you listen, Wicks. This eject game you're playing—you're playing my game, and it stops now!"

Reggie had me by the arm again. He led me around the corner into the boys' room and threw me in. I stumbled, but he grabbed me by the coat before I fell to the tiles. Then he threw me again. This time toward a stall. The door swung open, but I caught myself on the sides.

"What do you want, Reggie?"

With both hands, he took me by the collar and

brought me to the sinks. He had me so I was practically seated in the basin.

"What do you want?" I tried holding up my hands. My head was against the mirror.

"You're busted, Wicks. I made that game up two years ago. You know that?"

I tried shaking my head, but I couldn't, since he was pressing it to the mirror.

"Yeah, I made it up, but Zig shut me down."

"I guess you didn't learn your lesson?" I surprised myself with my own words.

"What did you say?"

"Nothing."

Reggie slammed his forearm into my neck. I lost my wind.

"You being a wiseass, Wicks?"

"What do . . . what do you want?" I managed to ask again.

"I have what I want. You. You stole from me, Wicks. Now I want what's mine."

"I didn't know."

"That don't mean shit! Ignorance is no defense. If you don't know the rules, you shouldn't be playin'. Give me what you made. Every last dime."

"No way, man." I surprised myself again.

"This isn't a negotiation, Wicks!"

Reggie lifted his arm and elbowed me in the face. No one had ever hit me in the face like that before. It hurt.

"Reggie—"

"Yeah, this is a shakedown!"

Another elbow connected with the other side of my face. I went down. Hard.

"Betting is not permitted at the Creek!" Reggie pointed at me. "Not under my watch. Not while I'm still doing my time here."

12.

ALL THE FACES were blank again. Expressionless. No one paid attention. No one cared.

The thrill was gone. Everything old was new again.

TEG had been a limited engagement. It had to be. Everyone knew it coming in. And when it ended—abruptly—there was no need to announce it. Or explain why.

Everyone knew. Everyone just knew.

I pounded my fist into the desk. This sucked. It wasn't supposed to happen this way.

I looked to Travs. He felt so guilty, but I didn't blame him. He didn't know. How could he?

"Look on the bright side," I tried telling him. "At least I didn't get busted by Zig."

But there wouldn't be any spring soccer because of my shoulder. And the cuts on my forehead were going to leave scars. I also was going to need glasses if the blurriness didn't go away.

Reggie souvenirs.

At least I stopped pissing blood.

I pounded my fist again. This sucked. It wasn't supposed to happen this way. I was out of business.

"Mr. Wicks, why isn't your notebook open?"

"Huh?"

"You think you're so smart you can just sit in here and not even open a damn book?" Nixon hovered above.

I rubbed my temples and smiled.

"You find this amusing?"

I shook my head. But not in response to her question.

"You think you're getting special treatment in here because of some cast on your arm and some bruises on your face?"

"I would never think that, Ms. Nixon," I muttered.

"What did you just say?"

I stared her down. "I would never think that, Ms. Nixon," I repeated too loudly.

"Get out. Get the hell outta here! Go sit in the office. I don't want to see your face in this classroom until I discuss with *both* your parents what you've been doing in here."

I no longer tried to mask my smile.

At the door, I stopped and turned. I acknowledged my classmates with a wave. They were going to miss TEG.

So was I.

Ms. Nixon, you haven't a clue what I've been doing in here. You have no idea, you old Crisp.

I wanted to say that, but I didn't. I did have a big pair for a soph. Reggie was right. But not that big.

Bullied

The Freshman

JORDAN COULD SENSE THE LURKING ATTACKS. He had developed the ability during his very first days at the Creek. Like vulnerable prey, he had learned the scent of danger.

This morning, though, his defenses let him down. This morning, he didn't see the elbow, and this time it wasn't only an elbow. This time it was an elbow-forearm combination. It sent him airborne.

The attacks had started on day one, like an initiation, but they hadn't ever let up. Now they were routine, a part of his Coldwater Creek High School experience.

What have I, what have I, what have I done to deserve this? The refrain from the Pet Shop Boys' song played in his head. *What have I, what have I, what have I done to deserve this?*

Nothing, Jordan thought. *Nothing at all.*

Then again, Jordan never did anything to deserve it. This sort of thing just *happened.* Second-grade soccer. Fourth-grade karate class. Summer camp. Always singled out. Always the same thing.

But this wasn't the same thing. *This* was something far different.

Amid the crush of students, he knelt in the hall against the lockers. He tucked the strands of stringy blond hair—which usually hung down over his face—behind his ears. Then he partially unzipped the jacket he always wore and massaged his shoulder and neck, the point of impact. How fitting, he thought, that the colors of his jacket were black and blue.

As the tingling in his arm and side subsided, he gathered his scattered papers like a child collecting leaves on a lawn. Then he stuffed them into the royal blue–and-yellow pocket folders issued to all incoming freshmen.

High school was going to be so different from middle school. He was going to turn over so many new leaves. That's what he had promised himself. Promised his mom, too. He was going to keep everything so neat and organized—his notes, his binders, his science labs, his art portfolio, his locker.

But in high school, Jordan quickly learned, many things were beyond the control of a scrawny fourteen-year-old. There was no point in even *trying* to keep some things neat and organized. There was certainly no point in trying this early in the day.

It was only second period.

The Teacher

MR. WALLACE SAT AT HIS DESK, grading the essays he had collected earlier in the day. He had assured his students they would have them back tomorrow, but judging from the height of the unmarked stack and the time on the clock above the door, that was not going to be. Not too long ago, he would have breezed through these essays in an hour or two, but now, even with his classroom door closed and his hearing aid turned down low, it was an effort to get through a third of them in that time.

For a while, it had frustrated him, his slower pace. But he had come to accept it. He could still do all the things he did ten, even twenty, years ago; it just took him longer. So what? He was still *far* more effective in the classroom than most, if not all, of his colleagues.

A paper clip bounced off his desk and hit him in the chest.

Mr. Wallace didn't look up. His hand, which gripped the red fine-point Sharpie, began to tremble.

A staple hit his forearm below his rolled-up sleeve.

He still didn't look up. He didn't have to. He knew whom he would see.

Andre Mills.

Not only had these encounters with Andre grown more frequent, they had also grown more unsettling. He didn't understand Andre. He couldn't figure him out.

What makes that boy tick? What makes him act this way?

Students never used to act like this. Not even the bullies. This was new. Video-game new. Post–9/11 new. Rap-music new. Collapse-of-the-conventional-family-unit new.

But all those theories—excuses—were too easy. This was more. That's what made Mr. Wallace afraid.

That was new too.

Another paper clip hit him squarely on the cheek.

Now Mr. Wallace looked up.

Andre sat cross-legged on a desk in the second row, reaching into the plastic tray resting in his lap and, one-by-one, throwing the staples and paper clips in the teacher's direction. As if he were target practice. As if he were a shooting gallery duck at a carnival game.

"Mr. Mills, can I . . . can I help you with something?"

Andre replied softly, too softly for Mr. Wallace to hear.

Mr. Wallace blinked hard. He knew exactly what Andre was doing. Andre was toying with him. In this case, playing with his poor hearing. Mr. Wallace had fallen for this before. Twice.

How long has he been throwing things? How long has he been in here?

He gripped the pen tighter, his trembling now having turned to outright shaking.

"Mr. Mills, can I . . . can I help you with something?"

Andre placed a staple in his mouth and spit it like a sunflower seed. "*Ain't* you gettin' too old for this, Wally-Walls?"

Mr. Wallace frowned. Andre wasn't the type of student who said "ain't." Andre spoke perfect English. Andre was bright, intelligent. It was why he was permitted to take AP Lit. Maybe that's what made his ways so disconcerting. The bright kids *never* used to act out like this.

"Mr. Mills, did you leave . . . did you leave something in class today?"

"Why you still here? Why ain't you retired?"

"Did you leave something behind?"

"Oh, wait. I get it." Andre snapped his fingers. "You don't want no part of the missus, do you? The missus drivin' you mad?"

Mr. Wallace couldn't keep his frown from deepening.

"Or maybe it's the other way around." Andre hopped off the desk. "The missus tired of *you*, Wally-Walls? She *makin'* you stay here?" Andre strutted closer and old-woman spoke, "'I don't wanna see you in my house till at least seven o'clock.'"

"Mr. Mills, you are—"

"She call it *my* house?" Andre's words came too fast.

"Mr. Mills, you are . . . you are out of line." Mr. Wallace's voice shook. "Your . . . your comments are inappropriate."

"Am I touching a sensitive chord?"

"Mr. Mills, do I need to get security?"

Andre smirked. "You really want to go through that again, Wally-Walls? Don't you remember the way them security guards looked at you the last time? Or did you forget already?"

A week earlier, when Andre had harassed him in the faculty bathroom, Mr. Wallace had gone for security, but by the time they had arrived, Andre was long gone, or at least safely hidden from sight.

"They looked at you like you was some kinda crazy ol' bastard!" Andre laughed and stepped even closer. "They thought you was losin' your shit. Just like everyone else round here. You is losin' your shit, *ain't* ya?"

Mr. Wallace stood up. This assault had gone on long enough. Slowly and unsteadily, he started toward the door, conscious of each step he took.

"You need some help there, old man?"

Mr. Wallace gritted his teeth. Just as he had fought wearing a hearing aid for as long as possible, how much longer could he deny his need for a cane?

"Go get security, Wally-Walls," Andre called. "Ain't no one gonna be here when you get back. They gonna think you some lonely old man lookin' for attention."

Another clip pelted the back of his head.

The Cheerleader

LIZ TURNED UP HER IPOD and folded her arms impatiently. Her father was late again. Practice ended the same time every day, but he still never managed to pick her up on time. It was bad enough she was a senior who had to wait for *daddy* to pick her up. Couldn't he at least be here when he was supposed to? Was it really asking for all that much?

She looked at the time on her cell. For a moment she thought about calling him, but she knew he never picked up when he was driving.

"What you doing, Lizzie?"

She jumped. Andre stood inches away.

"Don't worry about it," she replied.

"I'm not worried about anything except you, Lizzie. Waiting out here by yourself—don't you know the kind of trouble a girl can get into?"

"Shut up, Andre."

Where did he come from? Liz wondered. How did he sneak up on her like that? Usually, she *smelled* Andre's lurking.

She looked at her cell again and then out into the parking lot, wishing for the headlights from her father's SUV.

"C'mon, Lizzie. Take a walk with me."

"No, thank you."

"Why not? You know he's not going to be here for a while." Andre touched her hand. "He never is."

"Get away from me."

"C'mon. Let's go behind the school. We got time. You know you want to."

"You're disgusting."

Andre smirked. "C'mon. You know you want me underneath that cheerleader skirt of yours."

"I'm not a cheerleader." Liz pulled out her earpieces, but still wouldn't face him.

"Lizzie, you dance at sporting events." Andre stood too close. "You're a cheerleader."

"I'm not having this conversation with you."

She knew exactly what Andre was trying to do. She hated being referred to as a cheerleader. All the girls on the Rapids in Motion squad—which performed before and during football and basketball games—hated it. They were dancers. Andre was simply trying to get her riled. And succeeding.

"C'mon, Lizzie. Lemme play with your pom-poms."

"Drop dead, Andre."

"You know you want that. I make you hot. I make you wet."

"No, you make me sick!"

"Pretend I'm that little sophomore boy you've been flirting with. What's his name? Travis? Or pretend I'm Andy Addington. I've seen you with him. You tapping that, too? Does Reggie know about all your boys on the side?"

Liz gave him the finger, but still refused to turn his way.

"I know I turn you on, Lizzie. All us bad boys do. That's why you're hangin' with Reggie now. You never used to give him the time of day, but now with all his gambling shit, he *is* the shit. Yeah, you like us bad boys. Boys with an edge. Dirty. Rough."

"Drop dead, Andre!"

How does he know so much? About Travis? Andy? Reggie?

Liz didn't really want to know. It scared her enough that he did.

"I can see the steam coming out of you." Andre rolled his neck. "That outfit's so tight I can see the outline of your—"

"Go to hell, Andre!"

"You slut cheerleaders are all alike. I watch the way you thrust and grind." He ran his hand over his crotch. "Get on this. I'll give you a ride to remember."

"Is this your rap, Andre?" Liz finally faced him. "Is this how you get your *hos*? You sweet-talk them like this? You must attract quite a clientele."

"I attracted you."

Liz went silent.

At a party when they were sophomores, Andre and Liz had made out, but it had never progressed any further than that. It was also more than two years ago, long before she knew about Andre, and even longer before Andre had become Andre.

"C'mon, Lizzie. One time. For old times' sake."

"You make me ill."

"C'mon, Lizzie. Lemme stick my fingers inside you. Lemme make you come."

She turned her back.

"I'll make you come so hard you'll never think of Reggie or Andy or any other boy ever again." Andre jumped in front of her. "I know you want me. The things I say turn you on. I know they do."

Liz covered her face with her arm and bag and looked away. The things he said *didn't* turn her on, but they did make her think. How could they not make her think?

"Take off that sweatshirt. Lemme see your perky breasts."

"Do you ever stop?"

"I love the way they look in that cheerleading top. I can *feel* them. C'mon, Lizzie, unzip that sweatshirt, and lemme . . ."

At long last, headlights turned into the parking lot. Andre took off.

The Janitor

SALLY FELT THE BREEZE from the double doors at the end of the hall. She didn't have to look up from her mopping or turn down her iPod to know who had joined her in the empty after-school corridor.

"You missed a paper, Sweeping Sally." Andre walked up. "How can you possibly miss a paper?"

But Sally hadn't missed anything. Andre had dropped the paper. She had watched him drop it. She bent down for his gum foil and placed it into the plastic grocery bag hooked to the side of her bucket.

"Where'd you get your degree in custodial arts, Sweeping Sally?" Andre emptied more wrappers from his pockets onto the floor by her feet.

She bent down again.

"You know better than to be wearing that, Sweeping Sally." Andre yanked her headphones, pulling the earpieces from her ears. "You could get written up for that."

She fired a glare.

Her supervisor *had* written her up for it. Andre had seen to that. Andre was the one responsible for the formal reprimand. He had reported her and in all her years at the Creek, no incident had made her more furious. She did her job better than anyone, and after nearly two and a half decades of loyal service, how dare *anyone* question that she listened to music *after* school hours.

But that was how Andre Mills got off. By making lives miserable. He was a first-class punk, and when it came to first-class punks, janitors were always on the front lines. Always the favored targets.

Only, Andre's *punking* was different. It was the worst she had ever encountered in all her years. No student had ever taken it to his extreme.

Mr. Wallace agreed with her. He was one of the few remaining staff members who still actually spoke to Sally. The newer staff—the next generation—

walked by her like she was a locker, a mop, or a student. But Mr. Wallace knew all about what Andre did to her, and she knew all about what he did to Mr. Wallace. So if anything was ever to happen . . .

"You're a slacker, Sweeping Sally." Andre stood over her and smirked. "Slacker Sweeping Sally. Does your supervisor know that, too?"

The Freshman

THANK GOD FOR ALBERTO, Jordan thought. And double thanks they shared the same lunch period.

In this once-a-day venue, Alberto provided Andre with an alternative target. He was the distraction who averted the monster's eyes. Jordan felt indebted to Alberto. Which made him feel guilty.

But not guilty enough to actually do anything.

From across the cafeteria, Jordan turtled his head into his jacket, shifted the collar so that it partially hid his face, and watched.

Alberto seemed so pathetic. He *was* pathetic. This entire scene was pathetic. Straight out of a bad TV movie. Only this was real, and there was nothing Alberto could do but accept his starring role as the high school nerd tormented by the evil bully.

First came a pretzel.

It skipped by his table like a pebble on a pond. Alberto didn't look up from the foodlike substances on his Styrofoam lunch tray.

A second pretzel sailed past his shoulder.

A third bounced off his tray and into his lap. He brushed it to the floor.

Tell someone, Jordan silently urged.

Alberto could tell on Andre. Tell one of his teachers. His guidance counselor. An administrator. He could go directly to Principal Danzig. Or even his parents.

No, he couldn't. Jordan knew that better than anyone. Those weren't options. Not at all. Alberto had no one to tell. Freshmen, geeks, nerds, and the like never told. What good would it do? What could anybody do about *this*? In the end, they were just as powerless as he was. Telling only made things worse.

Next came a partially open ketchup packet. It hit Alberto's arm. He wiped away the red.

Fight back, Jordan wished.

Yeah, right. Like that was an option too.

The Pepsi can hit Alberto squarely in the cheek. Hard. Jordan knew it hurt. It left a mark. Soda ran down Alberto's face and neck.

All Jordan could do was watch this drama unfold from across the cafeteria. They were kindred spirits, he and Alberto, resigned to their role and place at the bottom of the high school food chain.

The Cheerleader

"I CAN'T BELIEVE you think I let him." Liz reached across the cafeteria table into Karen's bag of Doritos.

"If you really want Andre to stop," Karen replied, "there are measures you can take."

"I told you, he hasn't done anything to me, and he isn't going to either."

"Then why were you freaking out on the phone?"

"He surprised me," Liz answered. "I told you that. I didn't see him coming this time."

"*This time.* Do you even hear yourself anymore?"

"All he did was touch my hand, Karen. That's it. When I pulled away, he knew to stop."

"Oh, that's so polite of him. What a docile and gentle soul."

Liz took another chip and then wiped her Dorito fingers on a crumpled napkin. "Get those away from me. My uniform's tight enough as it is."

"Listen, Liz. Where I come from—"

"Oh, God. Here we go. Now I get to hear about how life was back in the sticks."

When Karen had arrived at the Creek last year,

Liz had been assigned to her. All new admits and transfers to the Creek were given a buddy-escort.

It was the only reason they had become friends in the first place. Liz and Karen would never have spoken a word to each other otherwise. Karen wasn't what you'd call cool, and she certainly wasn't the type of girl Liz's circle of friends welcomed into their fold. Karen was odd, with her not-from-around-here accent and her small-town, non-suburban attitudes.

Still, there was something about her that Liz actually liked. But, even more than a year later, Liz still couldn't quite put her finger on it. Of course, she wanted to believe it was more than the fact that Karen was extremely smart, and that they had had five classes together last year (three again this year), and that having perfect notes had instantly become a given.

"At my old school," Karen began, "if anything remotely like this transpired, the first thing—"

"At your old school," Liz quickly interrupted, "there were forty kids, not four thousand. There were two school buses, six teachers, and everyone knew everyone and everyone else's business."

"That has nothing to do with this situation or reality." Karen's voice grew louder. "No matter how you look at things, what he's doing is sexual harassment."

"Oh God, Karen! Aren't we being a little melo-dramatic?"

"It is, Liz. It's verbal assault. It's rape."

"Rape? Should I tell the police? 'Excuse me, Mr. Officer, a boy's bothering me.' Maybe that's *rape* back where you come from, but round here, that's what we locals call teasing."

"Well, in my book—"

"Lower your voice," Liz interrupted. She glanced about the cafeteria.

"Where I come from, it's much more than teasing. He would never get away with this."

"But you're at the Creek now, and it's a different world. The real world."

"I would never let him say things like that to me.

"Of course you wouldn't, Karen."

"A part of me thinks that deep down you must like it or something."

"We need to end this conversation."

The Fruit

SHANE STOOD IN THE HALLWAY amid the crush of students racing for their after-last-period-on-Friday destinations. The brushes and bumps and shoulders and elbows were of no matter. All that mattered was the purple-and-black graffiti emblazoned on his locker.

GOT
AIDS
YET?

The first two times this had happened, Shane had been frantic to erase the slur. At the time, not everyone knew about what had happened on the ski trip. Back then he still had hope.

But everyone knew now. It was no longer something he could deny or hide. There was no sense in even trying.

Which was why, this time, he simply stood and stared at the words on his locker.

"You want some help with that?" Sally asked, passing by dragging a recycling bin.

"No, it's my mess."

"I have some heavy-duty cleaner. It'll take that off in a sec."

"It's mine." Shane patted his chest. "I'll take care of it."

"Suit yourself, but in case you change your mind, I'll leave my closet open. Just make sure you click the knob so it locks when you're done."

The Freshman

JORDAN SAT IN THE CHAIR outside the door. He already knew this routine well.

When you visited guidance during drop-in hours, you received your file from one of the student assistants working the counter. Then when you entered the counselor's office, you gave him your file.

This was already Jordan's fourth meeting, but he still couldn't remember his guidance counselor's name. It had a hyphen. Dr. Something-Something.

Dr. Something-Something couldn't remember Jordan's name, either, but that was understandable. He couldn't be expected to know the names of the dozens of new students assigned to him.

At least Dr. Something-Something finally knew Jordan's face.

This is me in grade nine, baby, this is me in grade nine. The refrain from the Barenaked Ladies song played in his head. *This is me in grade nine, baby, this is me in grade nine.*

Words and songs always played in Jordan's head during his moments of greatest upheaval and unease. But not as a coping mechanism. More as an involuntary response to his despair. It wasn't something of his choosing. Nor was the selection that played on his internal jukebox.

As he waited, Jordan thought back to last year, to the high school information session, when a group of ninth graders had come back to his middle school to talk to next year's incoming class.

Jordan had wanted to ask *the* question to the five freshman panelists on the auditorium stage. How relieved he had been when someone else asked it for him.

"Do freshmen get picked on?"

"Not as bad as other places," the boy in the middle answered.

"What's done about it?"

"Nothing really," said the girl on the end. "You deal with it. It's part of high school."

Then the girl on the other end added, "If you find it's a problem, and I'm sure that you won't, you can always go to drop-in hours in the guidance office. If you have *any* problems as a freshman, that's what I recommend. It's a good safe first step, and most of the counselors are really helpful."

Jordan stepped inside.

"So what can I do you for today?" Dr. Something-Something didn't get up from behind his desk. He took the thin file from Jordan and motioned him to the empty chair.

"Not much." Jordan sat down. "Just wanted . . . just wanted to pop in. You know." He shrugged.

"Not a bad idea." Dr. Something-Something answered with a smile, but without looking up from the notes he had taken at their previous sessions. "We are planning on spending the next four years together, right?"

Jordan nodded. The song in his head resumed.

I found my locker and I found my classes,
Lost my lunch and I broke my glasses.
That guy is huge!
That girl is wailing!
First day of school and I'm already failing.

Dr. Something-Something looked up. "You enjoying the art elective we switched you into?"

Jordan nodded again.

"But what's with the jacket? Why are you wearing . . ."

"I like to keep it on."

"It belongs in your locker. You shouldn't have to be reminded of that. Is everything okay with your locker now?"

"Uh-huh," Jordan uttered.

"You're happy with where we moved it?"

"It's much better."

Dr. Something-Something tapped his notes with his pencil. "Your mother seemed to indicate you were pretty worried there for a while."

"She called you again?"

"No, just that one time."

Jordan shifted in his seat. "I wish she'd let me handle my life on my own."

"She's just being a mom. Making sure her son's okay."

"I'm okay. It wasn't that big a deal."

"Well, the Creek's a big place, and it's easy to get lost. It's quite a transition."

"Transition."

Jordan hated the word. It was the word of the moment, especially out of his mother's mouth. And each time he heard it, he wanted to scream. It's a difficult transition starting high school. It's quite a transition going from the top rung in middle school to the bottom rung in high school. Adolescence is a transition period. Ninth grade is the transition year.

Transition this.

He wanted to do this on his own. He wanted to

manage high school without her help. Why couldn't she see that her meddling was only making his transition more difficult?

Anyway, his transition wasn't the problem.

"You're managing to stay up on all your work?" Dr. Something-Something closed the file. "Keeping up in everything?"

Jordan nodded.

"Do you find the folders and planners helpful?"

"Very."

"Yeah, most freshmen seem to think so, and if you need more just help yourself." Dr. Something-Something patted the stack piled on his desk. "These bad boys really help you keep your house in order. The toughest part of high school involves learning to budget your time and staying organized."

"I think so." Jordan brushed some strands of hair from his eyes and tucked them behind his ear.

"Any other issues? Any problems?"

Jordan shook his head.

I've got a blue-and-red Adidas bag and a humongous binder,
I'm trying my best not to look like a minor niner.
I went out for the football team to prove that I'm a man.

I guess I shouldn't tell them that I like Duran Duran.

Dr. Something-Something inched forward. "I get the feeling there's something else you want to tell me. Something you're—"

"Andre Mills." The name just came out. Like the words had a mind of their own. "I don't know how much more I can take."

Dr. Something-Something's cheery "what-can-I-help-you-with" demeanor disappeared. "Well . . . what . . . what has he been doing?"

"Attacking me!" Jordan blurted.

"Attacking? What do you mean by 'attacking'?"

"Every time I pass him in the hall. I'm scared. I'm scared of what he might do. But I can't . . . I can't . . . I don't want to go to Principal Danzig because that would be tattling, and I don't want to go to my mom because she already thinks I can't take care of myself, and I don't want to tell my teachers because they don't know me yet, and it's really not their concern, and . . ."

Jordan stopped. He stared at Dr. Something-Something's grim expression. This was not a new conversation for Dr. Something-Something.

The Fat Girl

"HOW MUCH DO YOU WEIGH? One eighty? One ninety?"

Amanda reached into her locker and pulled out her chem text.

"Too many lonely nights on the couch with Ben & Jerry?"

Andre leaned against the wall, posing like a flirtatious jock. He did it on purpose. All his actions were calculated and deliberate. Exaggerated. Anything to make Amanda feel worse.

"Teenage obesity has reached epidemic proportions. You aware of that, Mandy?"

She pretended to check her contacts in her locker mirror. Her eyes were reddening and swelling. She was going to cry. She always cried. That's when Andre stopped. But never until.

"You weren't always this fat, were you, Mandy?"

Sticks and stones may break my bones but names will never harm me.

Bullshit! Words hurt. Words killed. No matter how many times she heard them. No matter how many times she was forced to endure them. On the playground. In the Girl Scouts. With the church group.

"Why'd you let yourself go like this? Don't you like yourself, Mandy?" Andre swung around so she could see him in the reflection. "Why do you even have a mirror? Do you really need a reminder of what you look like?"

She used to consider crying right away, as soon as he showed up, but she couldn't allow herself to give in like that. She had to save some face.

"C'mon, Mandy. Spare the rest of us. One image of you is plenty."

She went to shut her locker, but Andre's arm shot forward.

"At least wear some makeup. Show a little compassion for the rest of the world."

He flicked the mirror off its hook. It crashed to the floor.

The Cheerleader

KAREN'S WORDS FROM THE CAFETERIA had registered.

If you really want Andre to stop, there are measures you can take.

Karen was right. There were measures she could take. Which was why she was heading to Principal Danzig.

Zig would listen to her. Of course he would. The A-list females of the Creek—cheerleaders, fashionistas, dancers—all had pull with the principal. More pull than the honor students. More pull than the teachers. Even more pull than the parents on the school board.

It was just one of those things about Zig. One of those many *understood* things. Things that no one liked to talk about. Except for Karen, of course. She often wanted to discuss them, but Liz never allowed herself to participate in those conversations.

But because of her access and status, because of her privileged place in the Creek student hierarchy, Liz had come to learn things. Things that others couldn't know. Insight into some of those *understoods*.

In the process, she had developed an appreciation for the job Principal Danzig did. He was a great principal, running the Creek better than anyone else possibly could.

But that by no means meant he ran it perfectly.

Like everyone else, Liz heard the whispers and doubts. What really went on all those times he locked his office door? Was everything aboveboard? Did he favor some kids over others? Cut deals? Use students to get to other students? Just like everyone else, she didn't know for sure where fact ended and where fiction began.

But Liz knew better than most. Behind all those whispers and questions, she knew there were truths. Because she was in with Zig, and it was *understood*.

Still, Liz never questioned. Not when he pounced on minor victimless infractions. Or when he turned a blind eye to blatant, serious student violations. Because she knew better.

Until right now. Until today.

"People don't think you're doing anything." She sat on the sofa next to his desk, her feet draped over the armrest.

"Let them think what they want to think." Principal Danzig shook his head as he spoke to the stacks and piles on his desk. "They're going to anyway."

"Kids see you doing things all the time, Zig, but they're not seeing you doing anything now."

"You and I both know that's not the case."

"I'm not so sure."

"Excuse me?" He looked up.

"He shouldn't be allowed to get away with this. Any of this."

"Andre's a troubled young man. He doesn't come from a very supportive environment. To say the least."

"Why does that matter?" Liz sat up.

"I'm not saying it excuses it, but Andre doesn't have it easy. There's a long history of domestic violence in his family. His younger sister is chronically ill with—"

"Ask me if I care."

Principal Danzig swiveled his chair toward her. "You should care, Elizabeth."

Liz swallowed. She was wading in dangerous and unchartered waters. Sure she was *permitted* to speak to Zig with an edge, but even she knew this was stretching the boundaries.

"Zig, I don't mean to be cold. I know how you feel about every student being unique and having a story and I know that's your reasoning for running things around here the way you do. I get all that. But Andre is being allowed to get away with things. . . ."

"Elizabeth, Andre's an extraordinarily bright young man. Extremely intelligent. He knows exactly what he can and cannot get away with."

"Stop defending him, Zig! My best friends can't go to the prom or walk at graduation, but Andre can—"

"Hold on!" He cut her off. "Don't bring them into this. What took place on that ski trip with Nikki and Jo and everyone else has nothing to do with any of this."

"It does now." Liz tried to keep her voice from rising. "It has everything to do with this."

"No it doesn't." He rapped his knuckles on the desk. "It's apples and oranges."

"You won't do anything to Andre, but you'll ban my best friends from prom and graduation—"

"They were drinking!" Principal Danzig cut her off again.

"So you say, but you don't know that. They never left their room."

"Elizabeth, I know for a fact that each and every one of you was planning on drinking that night. I also know for a fact that the friends you're speaking of intended to engage in sexual activity. Those girls knew the rules."

"Zig, if you're going to start punishing people for knowing things, you're going to be punishing everyone."

"Elizabeth, you're pushing your luck right now." Principal Danzig rapped his knuckles again. "This is inappropriate. I'm through talking about other students with you."

But Liz wasn't. "Zig, I know why you don't want to suspend Andre. Because for however long you suspend him, once the suspension's over, you're right back to square one. He's here again. Doing all the same things. But you need to send a message. Like you did with Reggie."

"Elizabeth, I'm a principal, not a warden. Students here—"

"I've heard your speech before." She interrupted.

"Well, it sounds like you need to hear it again!" He suddenly yelled, smacking his open hand on the piles of papers.

Liz shook, but didn't speak.

Principal Danzig let out a long breath. Then he stood up, took the four steps over to the sofa, and sat down beside her.

"Elizabeth," he said, his tone soft, "students at the Creek are afforded greater liberties than at other high schools. You know that. I refuse to run this place like a police state."

"No one's asking you to, Zig." Liz's tone matched his. "But Andre's crossing the line."

"Elizabeth, I'm on top of this. Trust me on this one."

"Do you have any idea how many kids he targets?"

"Trust me on this one, Elizabeth. I know what I'm doing."

"People are scared, Zig."

He nodded.

"Not just students, Zig." She placed her hand on his shoulder.

He nodded again.

"Andre's a cancer."

The Teacher

MR. WALLACE FUMBLED IN HIS POCKETS for his car keys.

Where are they? Where did I put them?

It wasn't until he fished into his front pocket for the third time that he finally remembered. They were where they were supposed to be, where he left them every day since he had started misplacing them so regularly: on top of the driver's-side front tire of his car.

At this moment that meant they were beneath Andre Mills, who sat on the hood of his car, kicking his legs like a child on a swing, kicking them ever faster as Mr. Wallace approached.

Mr. Wallace walked up to his car door without making eye contact.

"You must really be slippin', Wally-Walls. How you goin' to open that without these?" Andre reached down for the keys and jingled them like he was teasing a dog.

"Mr. Mills, may I have my keys?" Mr. Wallace spoke to the window.

"You really think you should be drivin'?"

"Mr. Mills, may I have my keys?" Mr. Wallace repeated to his reflection.

Andre wrapped his fingers around the keys and held them in a fist. "'Course you can. But first we needs to talk about the grade on my essay."

"What grade?"

"Exactly, Wally-Walls. You didn't give me no grade. Why not?"

"You got a check."

"Everyone else got a letter. I want a letter too."

Mr. Wallace glanced back at the fading school. It was far too dark to be in the parking lot alone with Andre.

"Mr. Mills, if you're worried about passing my class"—he gripped the door handle with his trembling hand— "I can . . . I can assure you . . . you have nothing to . . ."

"Oh, I ain't worried 'bout passin' your English class. I just want a letter like everyone else. I don't want no check."

"Mr. Mills, I graded your paper."

"No." Andre hopped off the hood and stood close. "You *checked* my paper."

"If you're worried about passing my class—"

"You said that already, old man! Or dids you forget?"

Suddenly, for the first time in weeks—months—Mr. Wallace was bombarded by an avalanche of self-doubt: Was he forgetting things? Was he slipping? Was that why he had turned into such an easy mark? Had the forgetfulness and senility progressed that far? Had he become a burden to *the missus*? Did the security officers really think he was losing it? Had he lost it?

No! Stop!

This was about Andre, he emphatically told himself. This was Andre. This wasn't about him and his abilities as a teacher and person. That was only what Andre wanted him to think. Andre wanted him questioning himself. Andre wanted him intimidated.

Mr. Wallace was.

"We both knows you *ain't* failin' me." Andre stepped even closer. His smirk returned. "We both knows you don't want me in your class again next year. That is, if you still alive next year."

"Mr. Mills, is that . . . is that a threat?"

"A threat?" Andre laughed. "Come on, Wally-Walls. That ain't no threat." He laughed again, stopped abruptly, and then crushed the keys into Mr. Wallace's hand. "That's a fuckin' observation."

The Fruit

SHANE SAT ON THE FLOOR alongside his locker.

"I take it you know who's responsible for this." Principal Danzig stood over him, arms folded.

Shane didn't respond.

"Do you?" Principal Danzig maintained his soft tone.

"Who do you think is responsible for this?" Shane didn't look up. "Who else would do this?"

"And from what I'm hearing, this isn't the first time." Principal Danzig squatted down. He balanced himself with his palm on the wall. "Shane, if this has been happening on a regular basis, why am I first learning of it now?"

"Would it've made a difference, *Zig*?" Shane snapped. "What would you have done? Tell me. I'd love to know. I can't imagine I'm your favorite person these days."

"Shane, one thing has nothing to do with the

other. I want to know why wasn't I told about this after the first time?"

"Gimme a break, Zig. This isn't some junior wearing flip-flops to school, or some senior driving to school when he's not yet allowed, or some dress-code violation you punish with detention. You'd've asked me for proof and wanted witnesses and evidence and all that other bullshit. You know that as well as I do."

And nowadays Shane knew that better than most.

In the past, it was only something Shane had heard about from others. How Zig never addressed the real issues—fighting, stealing, cheating, bullying. How if you were ever forced to deal with slurs, taunts, and abuse, there was little sense in running to the principal. At least this principal. Even though school was supposed to be a safe place insulated from such behavior, Zig was someone who took a hands-off approach. He subscribed to the theory that students should deal with these realities on their own, realities they would be forced to face in the real world.

On the rare occasions when Zig involved himself in these situations, he never made things easy for the accuser. He required far more than simple claims and allegations. He demanded hard evidence. Which there almost never was.

Shane knew all this now because suddenly, all this applied to him.

Which was why Andre Mills could get away with what he did.

"Shane, something like this—I should've been notified. Immediately."

"Fine." Shane stood up. He looked down at Zig. "I'm notifying you."

"I know this is upsetting. I know—"

"Zig, you know who's responsible," Shane interrupted. "As a matter of fact, when it comes to me, *you're* responsible. You and your zero tolerance. You know who's responsible for *all* the shit that goes down at the Creek, but you still don't do anything. What are you waiting for?"

"Shane, I need—"

"What are you afraid of, Zig? When are you going to do something? When it's too late?"

The Janitor

SALLY TWIRLED THE MASS OF KEYS and then snatched the one to her closet from among the dozens attached to the spinning hoop. She had performed this trickery so many times that she could grab *any* key to any *door* in this manner. She had the maneuver down to a science. After almost twenty-five years, Sally had everything about the Creek down to a science.

Except for what to do about Andre Mills.

For the third time that week, Andre had urinated in her mop bucket. Of course, she couldn't *prove* it was Andre, so of course her supervisor dismissed her claim of harassment.

"Ignore it," he said, like he always did. "You're dealing with teenagers. What do you expect? High schoolers are gonna disrespect the custodians. It's a given. I did it; you did it; we all did it. Brush it off. It's harmless. Yeah, it's annoying and bothersome, but if you let it get to you, you've got yourself a bigger problem on hand because that's when they do it even more."

But this was even more. Even Sally's supervisor, who insisted otherwise, knew this was even more. But he was scared of Andre just like everyone else. That's why he had listened to the punk when he had reported Sally for listening to her iPod.

Sally placed the key in the lock.

She always opened her closet tentatively. She had to. Because of Andre. Andre had a key. He had to. Only he could be responsible for the vandalism she so often found.

Of course, she couldn't *prove* it.

But one time she was going to get him. She'd booby-trap her closet. Then she'd catch him. Then she'd hurt him too.

She turned the key.

She'd prop things up so that when he opened the door, everything would come crashing down. Bleach. Paint thinner. The bucket of ammonia water. The power sander.

She inched open the door.

No, that was asking for it. Taking too much of a chance. What if he wasn't the next to open it? Others did use the closet. She herself even gave other students permission. Like that poor Shane kid.

She peered inside.

No damage. Her closet was safe.

But she didn't breathe easier.

The Principal

"I NEED A FEW MINUTES." Principal Danzig poked his head out his door. He looked at the staff members seated in their cubicles outside his office. "Everyone, hold my calls."

He didn't wait for a response. He closed his door and locked it. Then he walked across his office, sat down in his chair, leaned back, and covered his face with his hands.

He hated these meetings. They always took such a toll on him. Especially when they involved a new student. Or a good student.

Karen qualified as both.

But this time around, Principal Danzig could blame only himself for the meeting.

"The next time you have a concern about Andre, any at all," he had said to Karen, "I want to know about it."

And she had come back.

"Sir, you should have seen what he was doing to this boy in the library," Karen had said. "It was awful."

Principal Danzig had listened to her entire account, and there was no doubt in his mind it was accurate. If necessary, he could even authenticate it. The library had closed-circuit cameras. After Columbine, most high school libraries did. He could almost guarantee her words matched the footage frame by frame.

But Principal Danzig knew better than to pursue that course of action. It wasn't worth the cost and energy. In his war against Andre, such a strategy wouldn't yield him any new ammunition for the arsenal. If anything, such a route would do more harm than good, raising serious and troubling questions: Where had the librarian been during all this? Why hadn't she intervened? Where had Ms. Nixon been, the faculty member on library duty? It was bad enough he had to deal with her increasingly out-of-control classroom shenanigans; he didn't need this on top of everything else.

"You've been here only a year now, and what you may not understand is that we don't get to choose all the students that attend the Creek," Principal Danzig had tried explaining. "Granted, most of the students arrive here through one or two of the feeder middle schools, so we know about them and their histories. But the remainder are assigned here by the district, and those assignments are based on geography and other criteria."

"Sir, what exactly are those criteria?" Karen had asked.

"I'm still trying to figure that one out for myself." Principal Danzig had chuckled. "In essence, every school is dealt a hand without the option of returning the unwanted cards to the deck."

"But, sir," Karen had pressed, "no matter how a student arrives here, when you allow abhorrent conduct such as this, you're condoning it."

"Karen, even though it might not seem like it, I'm truly grateful you're here today." Principal Danzig had maintained his even tone as he'd dodged the retort. "Bullying and intimidation are serious problems in high schools, and in order to deal with them effectively, we need more students like yourself to come forward. To step up. Just like you are right now. Because without it, it's quite the uphill battle."

"Sir, I have to be honest with you. I don't mean to be disrespectful, but what I don't see here is an effective response."

Bear with me. Please. I'm working on this. I just need for you to be patient. I need for you to take a step back. Let me handle this. I am.

That's what Principal Danzig had wanted to say. But how could he? How could he say that to a student who perceived herself to be in peril?

"I'm truly sorry you feel that way," he had responded instead. He had pulled his chair in closer and had placed a hand on her knee. "But when it comes to matters of student behavior, I have very strong beliefs. I know you're aware of that."

Karen had nodded.

"I'm a principal in charge of a school. I don't run a penitentiary. I afford the students here at the Creek greater liberties than at other high schools. I never have, nor do I ever intend to turn this *home* into a police state."

That's when Karen had blurted the words that still resonated in his office.

"Andre's targeting Liz."

"Elizabeth?"

Karen had nodded again.

"No. She hasn't said anything to me."

"Sir, please promise me you won't tell her I told you this," Karen had pleaded. "She'll never speak to me again."

"What is Andre doing?"

"Please promise me."

"I promise."

That's when Karen had shared what she knew. It wasn't much, but it was more than enough.

Now Principal Danzig uncovered his face and sat back up. He was close. Close to a resolution. Close to solving his Andre problem. Once and for all. He was just waiting for his opening. But he also knew he was running out of time. Learning about Elizabeth made him realize that more than ever. Something needed to give. Soon. Very soon. He heard the cries. He saw the concern. He felt the pain.

Principal Danzig let out a long breath. It was time again. He stood up and rubbed his face. Then he walked across his office and unlocked the door.

"Open for business," he said, leaning out of his office. "Did I miss anything?"

The Freshman

JORDAN HEADED UP THE STAIRS and turned the corner onto the landing.

Andre was two steps away, heading down.

Instinctively, Jordan hunched his shoulders, gripped the sleeves of his jacket, and braced for impact.

The force of the body check pinballed him from one wall to the other, but Jordan had prepared himself only for the first blow, not the bumper-to-bumper ricochet. His body crashed and crumpled to the floor.

I'm a loser, baby, so why don't you kill me. The refrain from the Beck song played in his head. *I'm a loser, baby, so why don't you kill me.*

Jordan grappled for his glasses, which had popped off his face. Why had he even been wearing them? He knew better than to be seen with them in the halls. Glasses were for classroom use only. But he had been rushing, rushing to finish copying down his home-work and rushing to get to his next class on time.

Andre's steel-toed stomp reached his glasses inches before Jordan's fingers did.

The Fruit

GYM CLASS. The locker room. Shane's new torture chamber.

Since returning from the ski trip, he had perfected all the necessary coping mechanisms: He organized and arranged every article of clothing on the bench by his locker before starting to change. He practiced getting dressed and undressed—in the privacy of his bedroom—in order to determine the quickest method. And he avoided *all* eye contact; in particular, steering clear of jocks, goths, thugs, linemen on the football team, and anyone who had an inkling about his sexual proclivities.

In other words, everyone.

"It should be your fantasyland!" Dex had tried to joke. "A room full of naked boys—what more could a sixteen-year-old flamer ask for?"

He hadn't found it the least bit funny. No, the locker room was hardly Shane's fantasyland. This was high school, where the fag was the target and where predators—skilled hunters like Andre Mills—attacked their prey at moments of highest vulnerability.

Today, Shane was in his T-shirt and boxers when Andre greeted him with a smack on the head.

"Checkin' out the boys, Fruit?"

"Only you, Andre."

"What'd you say?" Andre smacked him again.

"I said, only you, *Andre*."

Andre smacked him harder.

"You went to Zig, Fruit." Andre began twirling his towel. "You really think he's gonna do something? You really think he *can*?"

Shane stared.

Andre was wrong. He hadn't gone to Zig. Zig had come to him. Zig had shown up at his locker.

"Don't you look at me that way!"

But Shane didn't unfix his gaze.

At one time, he thought Andre was a narc. He had the perfect cover—the bully into everyone's business. But once Andre had started targeting him, he knew the brutality went too far over the line. Shane knew that all too well. He also had quickly learned that the brutality was only marginally less if Shane didn't get in a few shots of his own. Which was why Shane always insisted on firing back.

Shane still stared.

"I said, 'Don't you look at me that way, you fuckin' faggot.'" Andre continued to twirl the towel.

"Yeah, Andre. That's what I am. A fuckin' faggot. Disappointed I'm not interested in *you*?"

The rat-tails came in rapid-fire succession.

Snap. Snap.

First Shane's exposed right leg. Then his left.

"Asshole!" Shane screamed.

Welts formed instantaneously.

Snap.

The towel slashed his forearm.

A circle of boys gathered, laughing in amusement and groaning in agony.

Snap.

The towel slashed his arm again, blocking what had been directed at his face. Shane lurched backward. His foot caught on the leg of the bench. He tumbled to the tiles, clipping his head on the corner of a locker during his descent.

The Cheerleader

"GET OUT OF HERE!"

"S'up, Lizzie?"

"Get out of here. I'll scream!"

"S'up, Lizzie?"

"I'm serious, Andre. Get out!"

"Lizzie, Lizzie, Lizzie, I've never seen you like this. Relax."

"This isn't funny. Get out!"

"C'mon, Lizzie."

"I'll scream."

"I know you will, baby."

"Stop!"

"C'mon, Lizzie. Kiss me."

"Stop it!"

"You know how—"

"Stop it, Andre!"

"No! You stop it! Stop being a fuckin' tease!"

The Cheerleader

LIZ LEANED ON THE HORN and screamed and cried and kicked her legs, smashing them against the underside of the dashboard.

She had opened the car door and slid into the driver's seat, but before her keys were in the ignition, Andre had burst into the passenger side and locked the doors. He had reached over and quickly placed his hand on her thigh, where her dance skirt touched her leg. She had instantly smacked it away, but this time, he didn't relent. She had grabbed for the steering wheel with one hand and for the door with the other, but by then, Andre had forced himself on her.

Where did he come from? Why didn't I see him?

Liz wailed louder. The welts on her knees burned and bled, but she couldn't rub or massage them. She was still unable to un-pry her fingers from the steering wheel, gripping it just as tightly as she had at the moment when Andre finally bolted.

You deserved this. This is what you get for yelling at your father for always picking you up late. This is what you get for insisting on having the car. You brought this on yourself. If you didn't make such an issue out of everything, this never . . .

In the closed vehicle, Liz could still *smell* Andre.

The Principal

PRINCIPAL DANZIG CLUTCHED the note Mr. Wallace had taped to the back of his chair demanding an "immediate conference" to discuss an "item of grave importance."

The conference had ended moments ago, but Principal Danzig still couldn't shake the image of Mr. Wallace standing at his office door, staring blankly back at him. Looking old. Looking lost. Looking defeated.

"Damn," he muttered.

Principal Danzig now had a decision to make: Would he log the meeting? He created written records of all faculty conferences held in his office, never knowing when he might need those minutes. It was his etched-in-stone policy, and on several occasions, those meeting logs had saved him.

But this meeting with Mr. Wallace was different. Did Principal Danzig *really* want a written record of it? No. Not if he wanted to do what *needed* to be done. So if Mr. Wallace ever alleged or insisted they had met, he would just deny it. Members of the Creek community weren't questioning *his* memory.

He dangled Mr. Wallace's note and waved it like the white flag it was. Principal Danzig still called him Mr. Wallace. He referred to all his newer staff members by their first names, but he maintained the formality with Mr. Wallace. Out of respect? Out of habit? Either way, it would feel odd—even wrong—if Principal Danzig called him anything else.

"Mr. Wallace, kids are different today than they were twenty years ago," he had said moments ago.

"I'm aware of that, Mr. Danzig, but Andre Mills is not your ordinary kid. He's certainly not your ordinary bully. I think *you're* aware of that."

"I am. I'm also aware that we need teachers here at the Creek who are willing and capable of handling such troubled teens."

"And administrators, Mr. Danzig." Mr. Wallace had adjusted his hearing aid. "We need willing and capable administrators, too."

"Mr. Wallace, I'm going to say what I have said to you several times over these last few years. You need . . . you need to truly reassess your situation. You've been a valued member of the faculty here at the Creek for nearly three decades, but it is time for you to take a step back. It is time to take . . . It is time."

In the past, when having these conversations with Mr. Wallace, Principal Danzig hadn't been nearly as gentle. One time he had told Mr. Wallace he was "slipping." Another time he had told him, "his time had come." And on a third occasion he had even said that if Mr. Wallace didn't strongly and seriously consider his overdue retirement, they might both be confronted with a scenario neither one of them wished for.

After each brutal conversation, Mr. Wallace had looked more and more devastated and demoralized.

This time, however, Principal Danzig's softer, kinder approach was met with a different reaction—an eruption that still reverberated off the walls of his office.

"Principal Danzig, spare me your sugarcoated euphemisms. Once and for all, say what you really mean."

"I don't know what you're talking about, Mr. Wallace."

"Then I'll say it for you. I'm a senior teacher here who on four occasions turned down early retirement. I know that doesn't mesh with your faculty youth movement and the board's desire to cut costs. I am no longer wanted here. I am fully aware of that. I'm an impediment. My mere presence only makes a bad situation worse. But, Principal Danzig, after all these years, have a little decency. Show some courtesy. And by all means, be man enough to say it to my face."

Principal Danzig crumpled Mr. Wallace's note.

Why can't anything be easy? Why does everything have to be so difficult?

Then Principal Danzig started to laugh. At moments such as these, he had the loneliest job in the world. Most people hadn't a clue about what he had to endure on a day-to-day basis. It was a full-time job simply dealing with all the *other* stuff that went along with being a principal. So few had any idea.

Not that he wanted sympathy. He didn't need it. Nor was he going to get it. He just wanted to be understood. Like everyone else at the Creek. Like everyone else in the world.

But a principal isn't a figure that a community seeks to understand. Principal Danzig knew that. A principal is someone who is judged. By everyone. By each action and inaction. A principal is perceived as the enemy, the bad guy. Especially by the students. Which makes that perception the reality. A reality that is different for every student. Thousands of sets of eyes all seeing the same thing, but all seeing it differently.

And like the students sitting in judgment of him, the principal gets graded too. By an unfair system. Using imperfect criteria.

What percentage of students graduate on time? Didn't graduate at all? How did standardized test scores measure up against other schools? Which colleges admitted the students? How many students took AP courses?

That's how a principal got evaluated. That's what went on the principal's report card. Fair or unfair, that's how a principal was judged to be a success or failure.

But that was only the academic side of the ledger. There was also the behavioral side.

Principal Danzig was no longer laughing. Nor was he even smiling.

Suspensions. The measuring stick around here. How many suspensions did he issue? The more he issued, the poorer the job he was doing. At least in the eyes of the school board. At least in the eyes of those who assessed his performance.

Which was the reason he so often chose *not* to suspend. Suspensions made him look bad. Suspensions counted against him. Even when they were deserved.

But when a suspension also involved the authorities or resulted from an incident during an off-site school activity, all of a sudden, it was a whole different ball game. Those suspensions *never* counted against him. In the eyes of the school board, those suspensions made Principal Danzig a hero. A leader. The perfect man to lead the Creek.

Principal Danzig shook his head. It made no sense to him. None of it did. It was why he had stopped trying to make sense of it years ago. Still, it was why he *had* to report Reggie to the IRS. And it was why he *had* to come down on all those kids on the ski trip the way he had.

Striking a balance. That's what the job of a principal was really all about. Striking impossible balances.

Andre Mills was one of those impossible balances. But it no longer was about striking one. It was now about striking back. The time was ripe. All he needed now was the opportunity. But where was it? Where? He was tired of the pained faces. Elizabeth. Karen. Shane. Jordan. How many more were out there that he *didn't* know about?

The time was now. Far too many had become endangered. Students. Teachers. Himself.

When the opening appeared, he would pounce.

"Damn," he muttered again.

He tossed the note toward the trash and missed.

The Fat Girl

AMANDA SAT DIRECTLY in front of Andre in Mr. Wallace's AP Lit class. She always wondered why he was in the class in the first place. How could someone like Andre be permitted to take up a space in such a popular elective?

Fortunately, Andre was never there more than two or three times a week.

But he was here today.

"Lemme see your panties, Mandy," he whispered

in her ear. "Do you wear fat-girl panties? Boys' briefs?"

Amanda squirmed.

"You know I like 'em plump. I like porkers who squeal. Do you squeal, Mandy?"

She hunched her shoulders and squinted as Andre's words rose above a whisper.

"I bet you're still a virgin. I bet you'd squeal *and* bleed. You still a virgin, Mandy?"

Her eyes started to well. It was one thing to cry in the hallway. She could duck into her locker and hide. But she hated crying in class.

"Of course you're still a virgin, Mandy. Who'd wanna poke a nasty beast like you?"

Everyone could hear Andre now. Everyone was watching.

Do something! Somebody say something!

But Amanda knew no one would. For the same reason no one did anything when Andre tormented Mr. Wallace. And Shane. And Jordan. And even Liz.

They were powerless. As powerless as she was right now.

Her tears flowed. Just as they did when she cried every night.

Amanda hated high school. She hated Andre even

more. And at moments such at this, she hated herself
the most.

The Janitor

SALLY FELT THE BREEZE from the double doors at the
end of the hall. She didn't have to look up from her
mopping or turn down her iPod to know who had
joined her in the empty after-school corridor.

But these days she did.

Andre approached quickly. Like he was on a mis-
sion. Steps away, he pretend-stumbled into her mop
bucket. As it dumped, he added extra kicks so that
water splashed the bulletin board and spilled under
the art room door.

Sally didn't flinch.

"You need to be more careful, Sweeping Sally."
Andre wagged a finger.

She bent down for the mop still resting in the now
empty bucket. She stood them both up and wheeled
the squeaky bucket back down the hall toward the sink.

"You should oil those wheels, Sweeping Sally,"
Andre called. "Use some of your hair grease."

The Freshman

JORDAN LIFTED HIS FEET off the floor and placed

them on top of the toilet seat. He wrapped his arms around his knees and cowered. He knew all too well what was taking place in the stall to his right.

Swirlies.

Jordan no longer fought back. He used to. Then he learned it hurt far more when he did. From the sounds of things, Alberto had reached the same conclusion.

He no longer used the urinals either. Urinals hurt much more than toilets. There was no seat to cushion the blow. Whenever he went to the bathroom in school, he always used a stall. Apparently, Alberto had learned this too.

Jordan no longer took anything with him into the bathroom. He always remembered to empty his pockets beforehand and leave the contents with a friend or in his locker. But on those occasions when he didn't have enough time to take the necessary precaution, he would transfer his belongings to the zipper pockets in the lining of his jacket. He had already lost two retainers to the Creek plumbing system, and he didn't want his keys, wallet, cell phone, or anything else to suffer the same watery demise.

As Jordan watched the coins and Altoids roll by, he realized there were still some things Alberto needed to learn. He would. Eventually.

Jordan pulled his knees in closer and concentrated on maintaining his balance. He replayed the last few seconds in his head.

Bang.

Andre had kicked open the stall, smashing Alberto in the back. But Alberto hadn't even rocked forward. He had been bracing for this. *This* had become *that* routine. Alberto was now so prepared to endure the abuse that sometimes it no longer even felt like abuse. Sometimes it no longer even felt as if he were enduring.

Jordan knew all this. Without ever even having spoken a word to Alberto, he knew it. Because as soon as he heard Andre enter the bathroom, Jordan had done the same thing. A learned response. Like one of Pavlov's dogs.

Today Jordan was the fortunate one. Andre had selected door number two instead.

But Jordan still had done what he always did anyway. What he did each time he was the victim. During each encounter, Jordan would simply imagine he were somewhere else, and before long, the episode would be over.

But today, as he listened to the suffering in the

next stall, as he chose to do nothing and wait, all he could think about was his asthma pump. He knew Alberto was asthmatic as well. Did he have his pump with him? Or did it land in the toilet with his head and other belongings? Jordan always thought about his asthma pump, no matter where he went in his head. It was the lone item he still brought with him into the bathroom. He always needed it afterward. He kept it in his hand, clutching it like a drowning swimmer holding on to a life preserver.

Just like he was right now.

The Teacher

MR. WALLACE STOOD in front of the copy machine and rubbed his tired eyes. His glasses, on the shelf adjacent to the copier, danced and rattled as each sheet passed through the machine. The seemingly endless job was at long last winding down. Next week's assignments were almost all copied, collated, and neatly arranged on top of the radiator. Soon he could go home and rest his Friday-tired mind and body.

The machine stopped.

Mr. Wallace leaned in close to the control panel, expecting it to read CHECK PAPER TRAY or ADD INK. But the panel was dark.

He reached back and felt for his glasses.

The lights went off. The door clicked closed.

Mr. Wallace felt *that* chill.

The lights came back on. Andre stood steps away.

"What you doing in here by yourself, Wally-Walls? A man of your age—you shouldn't be alone. What would you do if . . . ?"

"Mr. Mills, do you think—"

"Do I think *what*?" Andre snapped. He stormed forward.

Mr. Wallace backed into the silent copier. He tried straightening the glasses he had managed to pick up, but he couldn't steady his shaking hand.

"Mr. Mills, I think you should leave."

"You think so, old man? What about what I think?"

"Mr. Mills, I think—"

"I think I deserve more than checks on my papers. I think I deserve letter grades like everyone else. I told you that already, but you didn't listen. What about what I think, Wally-Walls?"

"You don't belong in here!" Mr. Wallace raised his voice. "Now leave!"

Andre fake-tripped forward, knocking into the papers on the radiator, scattering them about.

"Oops!" Andre mockingly covered his mouth. "Look what I've done. What a shame." He stepped on some of the pages, tearing them with his shoes. "Now, I'd love to help you with your mess, Wally-Walls, but you know, I don't belong in here. I needs to leave. That's what I think."

Andre reached forward, ripped the glasses off Mr. Wallace's face, and tossed them behind the copier. Then he headed out, flicking off the light switch and slamming the door behind him.

The Freshman

JORDAN WASN'T GOING to school today. He couldn't. He needed a break from the torture.

He was going to snap. It was only a matter of time before he did. He knew he couldn't fend it off much longer, but since his mother had left before he had this morning, he was able to skip school today. Again. He could postpone the inevitable for at least one more day.

Jordan sat on his bedroom floor and cried. At night, his pillow consumed his cries. During the day, when no one was home to hear, he wailed and cried as loud as he wanted, as loud as he needed.

The Fruit

SHANE HASTILY GATHERED his belongings from his locker. Andre was approaching. They were the only two in the hallway and, quite possibly, the only two left in the school.

"What's up, Fruit?"

Shane didn't turn.

"I'm talkin' to you, Fruit."

"I know," Shane muttered. "Don't remind me."

"What was that?" Andre smacked the back of his head. "Speak up, Fruit."

"I said, 'I know,' Andre." Shane turned. "I know you're talking to me."

"That's better."

"Why do you like being around me so much?" Shane looked straight into his eyes and smiled. He never realized they were the same height. He wondered why that thought entered his head at this moment. "You have a crush on me or something?"

Andre grabbed Shane's shirt. "I'm gonna hurt you, Fruit."

"All this rage and anger." Shane was still smiling. "What's it all about, Andre? Some pent-up, latent homosexuality? You should do something about it."

"I'm about to, you fuckin' faggot." Andre shoved him into his open locker.

Shane winced as his lower back slammed against the metal catch. "Leave me alone, Andre." He stood back up and pulled his knapsack off the hook.

"Where do you think you're going?"

Shane slammed his locker door. "I'm leaving before—"

"Before what?" Andre hockey checked him back into the lockers.

Shane staggered away.

"I said, 'Where do you think you're going?'" Andre planted his hand on Shane's shoulder and spun him.

"Leave me alone!" Shane called, cradling his backpack and fumbling in the side compartment.

"What you gonna do about it, Fruit?"

"I'll tell you what."

Shane pulled out the box cutter. "I'm gonna cut your face!" He waved the open blade.

Instinctively, Andre jumped back.

Shane wished he had jumped back farther.

"You gotta be fuckin' kidding me." Andre smirked. He stepped back toward Shane. "You're pullin' a blade on me?"

"I'll cut you, Andre. I'll—"

Andre roared.

Smash.

The head butt lifted Shane off the ground. He flew into the lockers and slumped to the floor. Momentarily, his world blackened.

"Nice!" Andre hissed, as he hovered over Shane, admiring the pain and injury he had inflicted.

Shane wailed just like he had when Todd, Casey, Dex, Ms. Curtis, and Mr. Bratten had all gathered in that fateful hotel room. The blood poured down his face. He tried to focus on the figure looming over him, but the blood and tears burned and blurred his eyes. He felt around on the floor. Where was the box cutter? Had he used it? Had he pulled it out? He couldn't remember if . . .

"Don't you ever mess with me." Andre's heel stomped his fingers.

More wails.

Andre kicked at the box cutter. It slid down the hall.

"I'll kill you!"

Then there was silence.

Except for the familiar sound of squeaky wheels. Sally, with her mop and bucket in tow, had turned the corner.

The Principal

PRINCIPAL DANZIG COULDN'T LOOK UP from his notes, and when he did, when he summoned the stomach, he couldn't look directly at Shane. He could only look in his general direction. He counted over thirty stitches in the unbandaged wound, and the grapefruit-size knot protruding from Shane's forehead was easily the most grotesque injury he had ever seen.

The last time he had seen one of his students this beaten up had been the sophomore from Ms. Nixon's class. But that had been under an entirely different set of circumstances, and the damage done in that instance didn't even come close to rivaling what sat on the other side of the desk from him.

Shane looked disfigured.

"This happened Thursday?" Principal Danzig asked.

Shane nodded. "Thursday after school. In the hallway by the math rooms."

"Anybody with you?"

"I was by myself," Shane replied. "Getting my books."

"And Andre just showed up?"

"Uh-huh. He started getting on me like he always does."

"When you say 'getting on me,' what do you mean?"

"C'mon, Zig." Shane flexed his swollen and bruised fingers. His pinky still bore the impression of Andre's heel. "The taunting, the goading, the homophobic comments. Do we really need to do this?"

"Yes," Principal Danzig replied firmly. "We do. We *really* need to do this."

Because this was Principal Danzig's opportunity. He realized it yesterday when the details of the attack starting falling into place. He had waited a day to go over the incident with Shane because he needed a night to think, to sort things out. He didn't want to respond emotionally.

But he did want to respond emotionally. And forcefully. Principal Danzig most certainly needed to. After all, in some ways, Shane was right. He was responsible for what had happened to Shane.

Right now, Principal Danzig was merely covering all his bases. Right now, he needed to hear directly from Shane what school security, the school nurses, and Sally had all already told him.

"Tell me about the weapon." Principal Danzig walked around his desk and sat down beside Shane.

He placed his clipboard in his lap and exhaled deeply. "What happened?"

"I lost it, Zig. I did. I was tired of his shit so I pulled the box cutter."

"Now, hold up a sec." Principal Danzig put his capped pen on the clipboard and held up his hand. "He pulled the box cutter on you."

"No, I had it in my bag in my locker. When I—"

"That's not how it happened, Shane."

"It was in the side compartment—"

"No." Principal Danzig lowered his hand onto Shane's leg. "That's *not* how it happened." He paused. "Let's try it this way. Shane, I'm going to ask you a few questions. All I want is a simple yes or no answer. Are we clear?"

Shane nodded.

"Not a nod, Shane. A yes or no answer."

"Yes."

"Exactly."

Principal Danzig lifted his hand from Shane's leg and showed him the index card affixed to the clipboard. "I already have the questions written out. I'm simply going to check the appropriate box according to your response."

"Yes."

"Andre physically hit you, yes?"

"Yes."

"A weapon was found at the scene, yes?"

"Yes."

"Andre made the following statement to you: 'Don't you ever mess with me.'"

"Yes."

"'I'll kill you,' yes?"

Shane nodded.

"Yes, Shane?"

"Yes."

"All right, Shane. I know I'm being redundant, but let's confirm this one last time. For my state of mind. Andre physically assaulted you."

"Yes."

"A weapon was found at the scene."

"Yes."

"Andre threatened to kill you."

"Yes."

"Yes."

The Principal

PRINCIPAL DANZIG CLOSED his office door and checked the lock. "Have a seat, Mr. Mills."

Andre had been standing by the window behind his desk. He sat on the sill.

"In a chair." Principal Danzig stormed across his office to within inches of Andre's face. "Now."

Andre smirked as he meandered around the desk and slid into a seat.

Principal Danzig followed. "Game over, Wayne."

"That's not my name, Zig."

"Yes, it is." Principal Danzig stood over him. "Wayne Andre Mills. And it's Mr. Danzig or Principal Danzig to you."

"The other students call you Zig. Why can't—"

"That's right, Wayne. *Other* students call me Zig. You are far from a student." Principal Danzig pointed down into his face. "You attend the Creek, but you are no student. You're a cancer."

"Zig, I see what you're doing. I see—"

"And I see what *you're* doing. You're trying to push my buttons like you push everyone else's, but let me tell you something, Wayne, it's not happening."

"Whatcha gonna do about it?"

Smack.

Principal Danzig's open hand slammed Wayne between his cheek and eye.

PHIL BILDNER

"You just hit me." Wayne raised a stunned hand to his face. "You just fuckin' hit me."

"Whatcha gonna do about it?" Principal Danzig mocked. "Game over, Wayne. I meant it."

"I'll report you to—"

Principal Danzig lunged at Wayne. The chair toppled backward, and both crashed to the floor, Mr. Danzig landing on top, driving his shoulder into Wayne's head.

"Your assault on my school is over!" Mr. Danzig gripped Wayne's throat.

"Get the fuck off!"

"Game over, Wayne!"

Wayne gagged for air, but Principal Danzig didn't relent. He dropped his elbow into Wayne's windpipe, smashing the back of his head against the floor once again.

"Get—get off!" Wayne gasped and kicked. "You'll be . . . you'll be fired."

Principal Danzig laughed. "Who's gonna believe you, Wayne? The principal attacked you? In his office? What kind of lame-ass story is that?" Principal Danzig pressed harder. "You've got to be kidding me, Wayne."

"I'll—I'll call . . ." Wayne coughed. "I'll call the police!"

"Beat you to it, motherfucker. They're already on their way. They're gonna take you from the Creek once and for all."

"They'll see . . . they'll see what you did to me."

"Damn right they will! They'll see what I did to you after you attacked me." Principal Danzig drew back his arm and drove a straight punch into Wayne's nose. Blood burst from both nostrils. "I fought back, Wayne. Self-defense."

"Stop!" Wayne flailed.

"No, Wayne! You never stopped. Why should I?"

"Stop!"

"Game over, Wayne. I got you. You brought a weapon to school. That changes everything!"

"Bullshit! I didn't . . . I didn't bring a weapon. What weapon?"

"Nice try, Wayne. I'm not buying it. You brought a weapon into the Creek, and you used it!"

"That's a lie." Wayne coughed again. "You know it!"

"Wrong, Wayne. That's where I got you." Principal Danzig drove Wayne's head into the floor yet again. "You committed assault. You committed hate crimes. You violated civil rights. You—"

"I can't . . . I can't breathe."

"I'm not settling for expulsion, Wayne. You're going to jail!"

"Stop."

"Stop what, Wayne? It doesn't work like that anymore. You don't call the shots."

"Stop, please."

"I have evidence. I have witnesses. I have the goddamn weapon, Wayne. You're going to jail!"

"I can't . . . I can't breathe. Stop!"

"How do you like it, Wayne? How does the bully like being bullied?"

Therapy

A Day in the Life of Our Senior Year

IT WASN'T SUPPOSED TO BE THIS WAY. This wasn't what I had in mind.

All I wanted was to record Therapy, to tape our last session on the final Friday of high school. Why? A graduation gift. An audio yearbook for my friends, a podcast scrapbook of who we were and where we were. A day in the life. I was going to give it to each of them on prom night.

It would have been the perfect gift. One they would have cherished forever. In the future, when their brain cells were betraying them and their Alzheimer's was kicking into high gear, they would break out this souvenir and jolt some of those recollections back to life. Or perhaps ten, twenty, or fifty years down the road, when they were reminiscing with their kids or grandkids about their younger and wilder days, they would push PLAY on this snapshot day from our senior year that their old pal Drew Coletti had memorialized. And they'd be able to provide the next generation with a glimpse of what life was like for the not-so-typical, but typical, turn-of-the-twenty-first-century teenager.

That was the plan. That's why I went to school with my Sony in the pocket of my cargoes.

Of course, I didn't tell my friends I would be recording them. I wanted the gift to be a surprise. But more important, if I had told them, it would have completely changed the dynamic and altered what I knew was going to be an all-time great session.

Which it was. Lots of talk about the Creek. Lots of talk about life. And lots of talk about sex. Far exceeding all my expectations.

But obviously things didn't exactly go according to my plan. That's why there's this. While my friends were off having the time of their lives, celebrating their last days of high school, this is what I had to do.

Our last Therapy session. It's all in here. Every last word.

But what I say to you now also contains far more than that. Far more than what you could ever have learned from that thirty-nine-minute podcast.

Just like I promised.

This is the complete picture of us. Of who we are and where we are. Not just my bud, blazin', and biology friends. But all of us at the Creek.

8:48 a.m.

Brad: You blazin'?

Drew: No doubt. Wouldn't miss it for the world. Our last Friday at the Creek! You?

Brad: What kind of question is that? You know it. Who's Lookout?

Drew: We had this conversation yesterday.

Brad: We did?

Drew: You're not kidding when you say your short-term memory is shot.

Brad: Son, it's because of all this hydro we've been smoking.

Drew: Then, stop blazin'.

Brad: Now, that's comedy. You crack me up.

Jesse: Mornin', y'all. What cracks you up?

Brad: Your face.

Jesse: Good one there, Brad. Y'all blazin' for bio?

Brad: What kind of question is that?

Jesse: Well, I'm not. I'm friggin' Lookout and
Scribe for our last Therapy.

Drew: That so sucks for you.

Jesse: Y'all want to trade?

Brad: Sure, I'll trade with you, Jess. First let
me sign up for postgraduation summer
school and take an oath of celibacy.

Jesse: Bite me.

Brad: Is the little Jesse-Jess a little cranky-
crankster today?

Jesse: Bite me twice.

Brad: I'll take that as a yes.

Drew: Maybe Liz'll trade with you. You should
ask her.

Jesse: Right. No way is she not blazin' for
Hurley's on our final Friday at the Creek.

Brad: Our final Friday at the Creek. Son, I like
the way that sounds. Maybe Kevin will
switch with you.

Jesse: Sure. That'll happen.

Drew: When it's your day, you got to pay.
Those are the rules.

Jesse: But this is the last Therapy ever, why do
we need to—

Drew: Rules are rules. No exceptions.

Responsibility isn't something to be
bartered or bargained away. No favors, no
hassles, no—

Jesse: Spare me the friggin' rules-and-
responsibilities crap. We meetin' here or
the Bradmobile?

Brad: The lot. Gives us a few more minutes to
blaze on this historic day. And gives you a
few more minutes to hone those
surveillance skills one last time.

Therapy

OKAY, BEFORE THIS GOES ANY FARTHER, I need to cut
in. Since things took this turn for the different and
unexpected, I have to explain a few things.

Therapy.

That's what we called our daily rendezvous in the
Bradmobile.

Therapy was controlled chaos. Intelligent, controlled chaos in the confines of Brad's SUV, strategically and conveniently parked each day in the third
spot of the second row in the lower student lot by the
tennis courts.

Therapy wasn't some junior-varsity wake-and-
bake experimental routine. And it wasn't a bunch of

seniors acting out as a result of second-semester boredom. Well, maybe it was these last few weeks, but not at any other time. Therapy was so much more than that.

We had a system. That's why it worked.

Our system created this microcosm, a climate-controlled environment where everything had a place and everyone had a role. There was an order and a clarity that allowed us to experience and experiment without having to concern ourselves with the extraneous worries of everyday life. It fostered amazing interactions, creative thought, and impressive dialogue. It enabled us to perceive and see in ways we normally wouldn't and normally couldn't. As Brad once put it during one of his Stoner Dude rants, Therapy was "an oxymoronic odyssey that was disciplined and driven, yet decadent and vice infested. Adolescent antics done properly. Getting high right."

And it was.

Yes, our system was enabling. We knew that. It enabled our use of an illicit drug. We were always conscious of the fact that the only reason all this was possible was because of the marijuana. Without it our system could not have thrived or even survived.

That was something we all were cognizant of.

But it's not something we apologize for. Nor will we. There's no regret or remorse. We're above and beyond that.

That's something we're all cognizant of too.

Therapy also worked because it wasn't some everyday entitlement. We had strict rules and guidelines, and we adhered to them all. Participants—Therapeutians, as we tagged ourselves—had to maintain an A-minus average or higher in Mr. Hurley's fourth-period AP Bio class. Any Therapeutian who missed a single assignment or who received a grade below A-minus on anything—homework, lab, test, whatever—was automatically suspended from Therapy until the unsatisfactory blemish was expunged. The rule was an absolute nonnegotiable. It was also one we never had to use. No one ever missed a single assignment. No one ever received a grade that didn't begin and end with an A.

Therapy, in a nutshell.

Oh, by the way, after the conversation that Brad, Jesse, and I had prior to first period, I turned the tape recorder off. I had achieved my goal. I was hoping that conversation would serve as my introduction.

And it did.

Perfectly.

10:24 a.m.

Jesse: Friggin' Lookout sucks.

Kevin: Hey, you got to pay your dues. Rules
are rules. No exceptions. Responsibility
isn't—

Jesse: Save it. I already heard that speech
from these two when I got here.

Kevin: Then don't bitch, man. We all got to
do it.

Jesse: I said, save it. We don't all gotta do it
the last Friday of high school. So I can
friggin' bitch and be a bitch if I want.

Brad: Jesse, at this point, do we really need to
remind you why we have our very own
Office of Homeland Security?

Jesse: No, I don't need a friggin' reminder.

Brad: I still bug when I think about it. Zig
motoring into this lot and parking two
spaces over.

Jesse: I said I didn't need a friggin' reminder.

Kevin: We didn't spot him until he was
brushing by our blasted tunes and open
windows.

Brad: He didn't even turn around.

Drew: But as I've said on many occasions, I never bought it. Not for one nanosecond. It was too out of character for Zig.

Liz: Any of this coming back to you, Jesse?

Jesse: Bite me.

Liz: I'll take that as a yes. This is dead-ed. I need to repack.

Brad: I'd say go easy, but we won't be needing bud next week.

Jesse: How can you say we won't be needing bud next week? Are you high?

Brad: As a matter of fact, yes, I am.

Jesse: You wanna be friggin' dry for prom?

Drew: There will be plenty of bud around the last week of school. Always is. No worries.

Liz: This is really the last of our smoke?

Brad: We're not the only ones short on bud. Everyone I know is rationing. It's a school-wide crisis. A real drought emergency.

Liz: Better now than a few months ago. Can you imagine how different Hurley's class would have been? If I hadn't invented Questions, and we didn't have—

Brad: You invented? Liz, what's with the revisionist history? I invented Questions.

171

Everyone in here knows that.

Kevin: Technically speaking, I was asking questions of Hurley long before we turned it into a game.

Liz: We? Try I. I was the one who proposed the idea of asking three questions of Hurley and—

Brad: An *idea*. But that's all. I formalized it into Questions. I established the rules about quality and level of interaction. Someone back me up on this.

Liz: We all came up with that.

Brad: I did. Just like I came up with the rule that Scribe determined the winner.

Drew: I'll give Brad that.

Brad: Thank you. And while giving me my props, how about acknowledging yesterday's performance?

Drew: You did ask three solid ones.

Brad: Three? Son, I must've asked a half dozen questions and made a half dozen comments about meiosis and homologous chromosomes. Each and every one of them was of the highest quality.

Drew: Hurley couldn't keep up with you.

Liz: That's not saying much these days.

Brad: Even if Hurley had been on his game—
which I'll be the first to admit he hasn't
lately—he still wouldn't have been able to
keep up with my nuclear division
discussion.

Drew: Someone needs to pack a bowl.

Brad: Not yet. I have the rest of this J. Let's
smoke it before we reload.

Liz: When it comes to bud, we may be looking
at a major summer shortage.

Drew: Things are not how they used to be
around here. The students of the Creek
have grown far too dependent on one
source. It's a dangerous thing.

Brad: Glad we're getting out when we are.
Next year's senior class may be in for some
tough times.

Drew: It parallels our nation's oil policy. Doesn't
make for a healthy or stable economy. Too
precarious.

Liz: What are you babbling about? Since when
did you turn into an economics guru?

Drew: I'm not. It's simple logic. Addington's
Theory.

Kevin: Here we go.

Drew: As far as dealers go, Andy Addington's
Mr. Reliable. Price is reasonable, quality is
good, and supply has always been
plentiful. Plus, he's only a junior. He's got
another year.

Kevin: What more could a stoner ask for in a
dealer?

Drew: Exactly. That's why everyone buys from
him. But once a source is no longer
reliable—even one time—everyone starts
looking elsewhere.

Kevin: Then he should make sure he always
has plenty of ganja.

Drew: Exactly again. But here's the problem.
Everyone assumes that because his supply
has always been endless, his supply is
always going to be endless. That's fool-
hardy. So when he dries up, it becomes a
school-wide energy crisis. Which is what's
happening right now.

Kevin: The real question should be, *why* is it
suddenly happening?

Brad: Don't matter to me. Come this fall, I'm
going to be away at college, where the bud

will be flowing like water.

Jesse: Did you just say the *c*-word?

Brad: Yes, I said "college," sober boy. But in allowable form. So pipe down.

Jesse: I'm not so sure that was allowable form.

Brad: Well, I am. That didn't come close to violating the Moratorium.

Liz: Since I came up with the Moratorium— which even Brad would concede—I should be the one to determine if it was violated.

Kevin: Determine away.

Liz: Thank you. The Moratorium banned two things from Therapy: text messaging and the discussion of college. But throwaway college comments—like Brad's—are permitted.

Jesse: Whatever you say, Liz. But now here's what I have to say: We'd better have friggin' bud next week for prom. It's bad enough I'm missing blazin' today. I'm not losin' out next week also.

Drew: Relax, tool. Watch the lot.

Brad: Is that bowl ever making it up here?

Kevin: Chill, man. I'm up next.

Brad: Well, I'm type sober.

Kevin: I thought you were lighting that blunt.

Brad: I will, but not until after the bowl is
cashed. Now hurry up. I want to be so
wasted.

Kevin: You're waste product.

Liz: Play nice, boys. I don't want to have to
send you to your rooms without supper.

Jesse: Is the Bradley-Brad a little cranky-
crankster today?

Drew: Sounds like he could be to me.

Brad: No, he's sober, and he needs to be wasted. Pass me the bowl and toss me the
lighter!

Jesse: By the way, y'all, just so you know, I still
have that bad feelin' about today.

Brad: Now, Jess, just because you're perched
on Lookout this historic morning doesn't
mean you have to go and ruin things for
the rest of us.

Jesse: I'm serious. I've been sayin' it for a few
days. I feel—

Liz: You feel? Jesse, are you one of those who
feels O.J. didn't turn Nicole into a human
PEZ dispenser?

Drew: Ouch! Unnecessary harshness. Fifteen-yard penalty and an automatic first down.

Brad: That wasn't harsh. When you want to see harsh, let me know. I'll show you harsh.

Jesse: Y'all can mock me all you want. I'm just passin' along some friendly advice.

Brad: Here's some friendly advice: Don't eat yellow snow.

Kevin: Has there ever been a time when you were Lookout and you didn't have a bad feeling?

Liz: Kev might be on to something there, Jess. You have bad feelings every time you're Lookout. You said you had one last week, and come to think of it, you said the same thing the week before that.

Jesse: Fine, don't friggin' listen to me, but y'all should finish up early today.

Kevin: Sounds like it's a heavy-flow day.

Liz: Need a couple of Midol?

Jesse: Y'all keep messin' with me all you want.

Brad: Jess, you're the only person I know who gets more paranoid when you don't smoke!

177

Jesse: I know things.

Kevin: Here we go! Is this another one of your
hunches? Are we about to hear some more
of your astrological psychic voodoo
ramblings?

Drew: The Internet excursion gone horribly
wrong! Why would you ever share
something like that with us? You knew we
would never let you hear the end of it.

Jesse: I'm tellin' y'all, that stuff's real.

Kevin: Right along with the tooth fairy and the
Easter bunny.

Jesse: Y'all are having quite the time at my
expense today, aren't ya?

Drew: No doubt. The most fun we have in here
is when we're dissin' on you. You know
that.

Jesse: Glad y'all find it amusing.

Liz: We tease because we love you, Jess.
That's the only reason we torment you like
we do.

Jesse: And it's so much fun for me, too.

Kevin: Hey, in our defense, you do bring it on
yourself sometimes.

Jesse: Y'all are sad, you know that? You're

BUSTED

going to spend the last Therapy dissin' on
me? This is Lame with a friggin' capital *L*.
Kevin: We're lame? You don't want to start
down that road. You want to talk lame?
What about your need to constantly
swear?
Jesse: I don't anymore.
Kevin: It's like you have a disease!
Jesse: I say "friggin'."
Kevin: In here you say "friggin'," but when
we're out in public—
Jesse: I don't say "fuckin'" nearly as much as I
used to.
Kevin: Thank God! You were out of control.
Jesse: I'm not having fun right now.
Drew: Now, hold on. Let's give Jesse some
credit. These days it's far more "friggin'"
this and "friggin'" that, and far less
"fuckin'" this and "fuckin'" that.
Brad: Now we need to work on that lame
accent of his.
Jesse: Okay, everyone, I'm sitting right here.
Kevin: Jess, we're just trying to help. This is
constructive criticism, man. Next year you
don't want your new classmates thinking

179

that heavy Southern drawl of yours is some
gay-fem thing.

Brad: For the last month Casey and Todd have
been calling him Karen.

Kevin: Karen? Like that girl who moved here
last year?

Jesse: Hello! I'm in the friggin' car!

Kevin: Oh, shit! They do sound alike.

Jesse: Bite me.

Liz: Jesse, I think I figured a way you can put
your astrology to good use. Maybe you can
use it to explain why you never get laid.

Drew: Ouch! Another blow to the gut delivered
by Liz.

Jesse: It's not like anyone else in this friggin'
car has gotten any this week.

Liz: I haven't gotten laid in a month.

Drew: I'll sleep with you.

Liz: Been there, done that.

Drew: As I recall, you enjoyed yourself quite a
bit.

Liz: Oh God, Drew. The Big Bang was a charity
lay. How many times do I have to tell you
that?

Brad: I love how the two of you have a name

for your sexual encounter.

Liz: It was a one-time favor for a friend. My
slumming days are over.

Jesse: Now that's gotta sting.

Drew: Pipe down, sober boy. If memory
serves, Liz, you came twice.

Liz: Drew, it was two years ago! How do you
possibly remember that?

Drew: Considering the amount of bud I've
inhaled in my lifetime, it is impressive, but
the fact of the matter remains, no matter
how much weed a man smokes, he will
always remember losing his virginity.

Liz: Well, it wasn't nearly as memorable for me.

Brad: Is that how it works, Liz? After a while, do
the sexual experiences all just blur into one
another?

Liz: No, Brad. I remember the ones worth
remembering.

Jesse: That's gotta sting again.

Liz: Drew was the virgin, not me.

Drew: You offered to sleep with me.

Brad: You offered to sleep with Drew?

Liz: He needed to have his cherry popped. So
I offered.

Drew: Every teenage boy's wet dream come
   true.

Brad: You offered?

Liz: Can I finally tell everyone about the
   arrangement?

Brad: What arrangement?

Drew: Sure, it's the last Therapy. Go for it.

Brad: What are you two talking about?

Liz: Before we slept together, we made up
   some ground rules.

Kevin: Rules?

Liz: We wanted to make sure we stayed
   friends.

Kevin: This sounds so pathetic already.

Brad: No wonder they never said anything until
   now.

Kevin: I want to hear these rules.

Liz: They were basic. Three commonsense
   ground rules.

Drew: First, it was a one-time thing. No second
   helpings. No matter how much fun we had.

Liz: Second, no kissing and telling, even
   though everyone ended up finding out that
   we did it anyway.

Drew: And no judgments.

Liz: The last rule was more for Drew. He
    insisted on that.

Drew: No doubt. Up to then my sexual
    experience consisted of staring at endless
    hours of online porn. This wasn't virtual
    anymore. This was the real deal. I didn't
    know what the hell I was doing or what the
    hell was going to happen.

Liz: We kept to the plan, stayed best friends,
    end of story. Next topic.

Kevin: Hey, Liz, maybe that's where we went
    wrong. Maybe we should have had rules
    also.

Liz: Why would we have had rules? We were
    going out.

Kevin: I'm just saying. It was the first time for
    both of us and—

Liz: We broke up right after.

Kevin: No, we slept together three more times.

Liz: Twice. Don't exaggerate.

Drew: And then you two didn't speak to each
    other for an entire summer. That was so
    much fun for the rest of us.

Kevin: So here's my thought: Why don't we
    have sex again? Right the wrong.

Liz: Kevin, my days of sleeping with one-
    minute men—or should I say, one-minute
    boys—are behind me.

Kevin: Hey, I admit, when we did it, I blew my
    load mad quick.

Liz: I don't need to be reminded.

Kevin: Now, be fair, Liz. If you're going to
    sweat me in front of my boys, I need to be
    afforded the opportunity to respond.

Liz: Fine. Just get it over with as quickly as you
    did when we did it.

Kevin: Permit me to fill you in on some truths
    about male sexuality: The first time a guy
    gets laid, maybe even the first few times he
    gets laid, one of the following will occur: (a)
    he's going to come before he gets his
    rubber on, (b) he's going to come in less
    than thirty seconds, or (c) he's not going to
    be able to get a hard-on. Any guy who tells
    you differently is (d) a liar.

Liz: Thanks for the lesson.

Brad: I need to say something. Time for the
    voice of reason to interject his wisdom. Do
    you all hear yourselves? Things don't have
    to be this complicated. Ever. Just do what I

do. Stick to jerking off. It's so much easier and hassle-free.

Drew: No fear of being rejected.

Jesse: Unless you can't get it up for yourself. That would friggin' suck.

Brad: Don't get me wrong; I love hooking up, but jerking off is way more convenient and efficient.

Liz: Do you still insist on your riding-the-bed technique?

Jesse: Humping your friggin' pillow or whatever you do is not way more convenient or efficient.

Brad: Works for me.

Jesse: When I need to rub one out, I don't need props or accessories. I can walk into a bathroom stall and take care of business. I can even whip it out while I'm driving.

Drew: Now that's what I call multitasking!

Jesse: I've perfected a variety of masturbatory methodologies.

Brad: Son, you'd better have. No one else is going to do it for you.

Jesse: None of which require friggin' pillows or mattresses. In fact, I'm proud to say I'm now an ambidextrous masturbator.

Drew: That means you go both ways?

Jesse:No, that means I'm equally talented with either hand. When it comes to the masturbatory arts, I've achieved a level of mastery.

Liz: If I didn't know better, I'd say there's money to be made in this. Set up a web-cam, create a site, upload some video, and charge visitors to watch some of your expert exhibitions. Demonstrate your prowess to the world.

Jesse: Who says I'm not doin' that already?

Drew: But you're limited to one venue with a webcam.

Jesse: I'm workin' on that.

Drew: Discriminating viewers these days want to see you perform in a variety of places. The beach. School.

Jesse: The movies. The food court.

Drew: Yes, restaurants. Good one, Jesse.

Jesse: The other day I shot this load that—

Liz: Shut up! You're all so disgusting. I'm sorry I ever mentioned the webcam and video thing. You're not normal.

Drew: You're right. We're not normal. We're
     intelligent.

Liz: Intelligent? Then why do you always end
     up talking about jerking off? And why do
     you always insist on getting so dirty and
     graphic?

Kevin: Seems pretty obvious to me. Our
     favorite topic of discussion is masturbation.
     Of course things are going to get graphic.

Drew: True, true. But I think there's more to it
     than that. We get as graphic as we do
     because we can. That's why it's always so
     no-holds-barred.

Kevin: What's your point?

Drew: My point is—now, hear me out—it's the
     last therapy so grant me a little ranting
     leeway.

Kevin: Just go.

Drew: We're teenagers. Everything is sex and
     sexuality. It dominates the thought process,
     and all those thoughts lead to questions.
     Lots of questions. But what we have in
     here—this system of ours—is a forum for
     answers. Real questions. Real discussions.
     Real answers.

187

Kevin: You're still stating the obvious. We've
been through this hundreds of times.

Drew: All I'm saying is adults never had this.
Even kids today don't have what we have
here. Except online, but that doesn't count.
It's not the same. Those interactions are
cloaked conversations; it's pseudodialogue
from behind a computer screen. Ours is
real, face-to-face, and looking people in
the eye. That's why we talk like we do.

Kevin: If you say so. I'll stick with we're
teenage boys.

Liz: I'm not.

Brad: Liz, you're one of the guys in here. You
know that.

Liz: Brad, if you weren't holding the bowl and
the spliff right now, I'd smack you silly.

Jesse: Listen to Liz. Bullying the boys.

Liz: I am not one of you guys. I would never
say some of the things that come out of
your mouths.

Drew: No? You don't think you say some pretty
over-the-top things?

Liz: I do, but I never go as far as you and
Kevin.

Jesse: Actually, you have, Liz. You've gone friggin' all the way with both of 'em.

Liz: One more comment like that and for the rest of your life you're going to have to explain to people why in your prom and graduation photos you have cuts and bruises all over your face.

Jesse: Listen to Liz, still talking the tough and bullying the boys.

Liz: Shut up and watch the lot!

Brad: Speaking of bullies, any news on Andre?

Kevin: Far as I know, he never made bail. He wouldn't take a plea.

Jesse: That boy is friggin' nuts.

Kevin: Whenever I hear his name, my head always goes right to that freshman kid.

Brad: That skinny blond kid?

Kevin: Yeah, I think his name is Jordan.

Liz: Can we please not discuss Andre?

Kevin: Man, every time that kid stepped into the hallway, he was running the gauntlet. I saw Andre level him at least a dozen times. He always seemed to find him on the stairs.

Brad: I walked in on Andre and that kid in the

bathroom one time, and all I have to say is, I still don't want to know what Andre was doing to him in that stall.

Drew: That kid is damaged goods. Someone needs to catch on to that. Real fast.

Liz: I said, can we please not talk about Andre? Do we have to contaminate our last session like this?

Brad: This thing's burning too fast.

Kevin: We should've just stuck with the bowl.

Brad: Son, it's our last Therapy; we had to smoke one of these.

Kevin: Then, no one's holding it for five tokes. Puff and pass, people.

Brad: And pack another bowl.

Liz: At your service. Already packed.

Jesse: If y'all kill the bud, I'm gonna kill some-one.

Liz: I got the bag now. I'll make sure we don't kick it.

Jesse: No, I'll take the friggin' bag.

Liz: Here.

Jesse: Jeez, we need bud in a bad way.

Brad: Let's go back to Andre.

Liz: Let's not.

Jesse: Liz, if you don't want to talk about
Andre, we can always talk 'bout your prom
date. Have you made up your mind?

Liz: Go to hell, Jess.

Jesse: Who's it goin' to be? Reggie? Mr.
Addington? Your little boy toy, Travis? Or
some mystery man behind door number
four?

Liz: You really do want to get hurt today, don't
you?

Jesse: What about Drew or Kev for old times'
sake?

Brad: Y'all remember what Andre used to do
to that Amanda girl?

Liz: Stop!

Drew: What's the matter?

Liz: I don't want to talk about Andre.

Kevin: What's the big deal? He's out—

Liz: I can't.

Drew: You can't. Liz, what is it?

Liz: If I tell you something—

Drew: Tell us what?

Liz: I need to tell you something, but after I tell
you, you have to promise not to make a big
deal of it.

Drew: That depends.

Liz: I'm serious.

Kevin: What is it?

Liz: You can't be mad that I didn't tell you. I'm only telling you now because it's the last Therapy, and I'll go insane if I . . . Look, I have to come clean about something, and if I don't do it now, I never will.

Drew: Liz, you're starting to scare us a little.

Liz: Just let me get this off my chest.

Kevin: Hey, that's one fine chest, it should be noted.

Liz: No judgments. I'm serious.

Brad: Never. This is Therapy.

Liz: Promise?

Brad: It has to do with Andre?

Liz: I was . . . I was one of his victims.

Drew: What? How come you never said anything?

Liz: No judging.

Drew: I'm not judging, I'm asking.

Jesse: Y'all, let her speak.

Drew: Who knew about this?

Liz: Karen's the only one who knew. She went to Zig about it behind my back.

Jesse: That's why you never let her join us in
　　　Therapy?

Liz: That's exactly why. I didn't trust her.

Drew: How did I miss this? How did we not
　　　know?

Liz: You didn't know to look, and considering
　　　my relationship with Zig, I should've been
　　　Andre-proof.

Kevin: Zig came to you after Karen spoke to
　　　him?

Liz: The same day.

Drew: When was this?

Kevin: It had to have been a while ago.

Liz: I can't believe I ever fooled around with
　　　him. For me, that's been the worst part of
　　　all.

Drew: That was years ago, Liz.

Liz: I know, but seeing the way he is now . . .

Drew: A screw is loose with that boy. That's
　　　what had everyone around here so freaked.
　　　That's Zig too. Why he finally pounced the
　　　way he did.

Jesse: Are you okay now?

Drew: What exactly did he do to you?

Liz: I don't want to go there.

Drew: Is that the reason you're smoking as
     much as you are?

Liz: *What?*

Brad: Son, where did that come from? You
     know better than that.

Drew: It's true, Liz. You are. You know you are.

Brad: Drew, when it comes to smoking up, we
     don't—

Drew: I know it's the last thing you want to
     hear, but it's something I've been wanting
     to say for a while.

Liz: I don't think you should go there.

Drew: Liz, you've been smoking too much.
     There, I said it. Spoke the forbidden words.

Brad: And now I'm stepping in. Stop, Drew.

Drew: Your pot smoking these last couple
     months has been affecting you, and not in
     a good way.

Brad: Drew, uncool!

Drew: I'm hoping it'll pass, and I'm pretty sure
     once school starts up in the fall it will, but I
     just—

Brad: Stop!

Drew: Just be careful.

Brad: Drew, we've never sat in judgment of

one another in here, especially about blazin', and we're not starting now.

Kevin: Hey, I say we find another subject. Next topic.

Brad: Fast!

Kevin: Hurley. Let's talk about Hurley.

Brad: Yes, Hurley.

Kevin: What's up with him these days?

Brad: Well, he's not ending things on a high note like we are, pun intended.

Kevin: He looks like he hasn't slept in days.

Liz: Do you think he's healthy? He's never been this much of a brain drain.

Drew: Hurley's burned. Just another teacher Crisp. Stick a fork in him; he's done.

Liz: Yeah, but even by Crisp standards, something's off with Hurley.

Drew: And once again I need to go on record and say I take etymological issue with those sophs in Nixon's class who think they came up with the word. "Crisp" *is* my word. Their claims of ownership are false and erroneous.

Kevin: Hey, we should do like those sophs in

Nixon's class. Play Questions for money.
Like their Ejection Game. Make things extra
interesting this last day. Scribe can collect
the bets and make the payouts.

Liz: What's the Ejection . . . Oh, that's what
they called it. I knew that.

Kevin: You of all people should know that, Liz,
considering your intimate connections.
Travis, Reggie—

Liz: Shut up, Kev. Don't start.

Kevin: Hey, I'm just making an observation.

Liz: If I have to, I'll beat you down too.

Kevin: Liz, I heard Reggie has a two-inch
penis. Is that about right?

Liz: Come to think of it, Kev, that is about right.
It's noticeably bigger than yours.

Drew: Ouch.

Kevin: I heard Travis was raking in mad dough.
Pulling in a few hundred a week. No
wonder Reggie shut him down. He gave
that boy a beating.

Drew: I heard he needs more surgery on his
shoulder.

Liz: Kid learned his lesson. That's for damn
sure.

Drew: And I'm sticking to my theory that it
    wasn't Reggie.

Kevin: Your conspiracy theory?

Drew: No doubt.

Kevin: Man, you've been watching way too
    much SCI FI Channel.

Drew: Say what you want, but I'm sticking to
    what I've said all along. Zig ordered that
    hit. You believe what you want.

Jesse: I believe you, Drew. I like the theory.

Drew: It makes complete sense. Zig's had
    Reggie's balls in a vise ever since he
    busted him. I guarantee he calls on him for
    favors all the time. He told him to rough
    that kid up and shut him down. I bet he
    even told him where and when to do it so
    no one would see. Why do you think
    Reggie's suddenly allowed to walk at
    graduation all of a sudden?

Kevin: That's not the reason. Reggie's walking at
    graduation because if Zig banned him, he
    would have to ban half the National Honor
    Society after what happened on the ski trip.

Drew: I'll give you that, but Zig hates going
    after kids like Reggie. It's not his way.

That's why he worked out an alternative.

Jesse: Imagine if Zig had ever come after us.
Tried shutting us down.

Liz: Shut up! We don't even joke.

Jesse: He could've. Our activities aren't
dissimilar.

Liz: Don't say such things.

Brad: Our activities aren't dissimilar? What are
you talking about?

Jesse: Wake up, stoner. Illegal activities taking
place on school grounds and carrying over
into the classroom—you don't think there's
a correlation?

Kevin: Hey, the last thing in the world we'd
want at this point is Zig coming after our
Therapeutic operations. We'd be done.

Liz: Can we really not talk this way?

Jesse: Why, Liz? Is it giving you a bad feeling?
Do you sense something?

Liz: Yes, I do. I sense you're not going to live
to see graduation if you keep it up.

Principal Edward Danzig

HOW AM I DOING SO FAR, ZIG? You getting what you
want?

I know you are. This is what you thrive on. These are the data points you crave. Because this all pertains to the mind-set of the Creek, and more than anything, that's what you want to know. How your student body is thinking. What your student body is thinking.

I haven't told you nearly everything yet. We both know that. But I'm getting there. Don't worry. I made you a promise. It's all in here. You just have to keep listening. But that's not an issue for you. That's a given. You find this riveting.

But first, Principal Danzig, I want you to understand just how much I know and how I know what I know and why we were able to shake hands on this arrangement. It's time to set the record straight. Time to shed some light.

When you're one of the smart ones, high school gets pretty tedious at times. That's the reality when you're intelligent. So I needed a challenge. I needed to find a constructive, productive, and fulfilling way to use my time.

I chose you.

I began observing you. I started during the second half of freshman year. I didn't tell any of my friends about it until this year, and when I did, they all had the identical reaction. They wanted me to consider seeking professional help. They also wanted me to get a life.

That is, until I started sharing my findings with them. They were stunned. They had no idea. The best and the brightest the Creek had to offer knew virtually nothing about how you ran things.

I know that's exactly the way you want things, Zig, but I felt an obligation to change that. At least with my inner circle.

Once we started Therapy, I made it a point to fully educate my friends. I needed the Therapeutians to know what I knew. Almost instantly they recognized the futility of trying to refute, discount, or dismiss any of my three years' worth of research. My once-skeptical friends were left with no other reasonable option than to respect and revere your accomplishments and authority. Like I do.

I see you in an amazing light, Zig. I think you're a genius. Living proof that a brilliant high school administrator is not a contradiction in terms. You get it. You know what it really takes to run a twenty-first-century public high school. And you know me well enough to know that I'm not just saying this to earn brownie points or get in your good graces.

Not at this point, anyway.

Zig, I'm constantly confounded by the things you're able to find out. Like Questions. I still have no idea how you found out some of the details you did. But eventually I will learn. You can count on that.

It's all about information for you. Intelligence gathering. In order to run the Creek, you need to know, and in order to know, you're willing to do what's required. That which is necessary. The man who presides over the Creek is willing to do whatever it takes, and sometimes that means stretching the limits of propriety. Sometimes that means extending the boundaries of acceptability. Sometimes that means utilizing approaches considered by others to be strong-armed and unethical. Brokering deals, forging alliances, enlisting the services of informants, cultivating strategic relationships, and establishing channels and back channels.

I know such tactics often ruffle feathers and make enemies. Many disapprove of your above-the-law approach. But you're not deterred. You know those in power are always going to have detractors.

You pick your battles wisely too. That's what you do better than anything else. You prefer the high-profile ones. Like the ones involving gambling, shoplifting, and bullying. Where examples can be made. Where decisive and unambiguous messages can be delivered to an entire student body. And it's during these times that you fortify your position as leader of the Creek. You place your finger on all the beating pulses. That's how you maintain your command and control.

You invest so much energy in your craft. It is a craft. One requiring great patience and skill. One you have mastered.

Like what you have with Sweeping Sally.

She's the best example I can provide to you. Always meandering by at the right time. Twirling her keys so nonchalantly. I'm not fooled. Never was. She's the eyes and ears of the Creek, and ironically, she never even has to actively seek out the information she knows. Most of the time it's told to her by the careless whispers of unsuspecting adolescents. But not me. The moment Sweeping Sally entered my field of view, I always knew to push PAUSE. The gate at the railroad crossing went down. I waited.

It was one of the first things I ever learned at the Creek, and it made my four-year stay here so much simpler. Whenever I wanted to find out what was really going on, I went to Sweeping Sally. She was always my first source. She knew. And for just a few dollars, more often than not, she'd tell me far more than I needed to know.

So I'm wondering, how much does she cost you? I know she has to. I know Sweeping Sally. How much cash do you slip her under the table? I know how much she cost me.

Don't worry, Zig. What I've learned—what I know—doesn't get shared. It's not for public consumption. That wouldn't be fair to you. It would undermine your authority, and that's not what I want.

You realize that, Zig. I know you do.

10:49 a.m.

Drew: I've got a hypothetical question.

Kevin: We've now reached the pseudo-intellectual portion of today's final program.

Drew: Here's the situation. You're a parent and—

Kevin: Man, I don't like this already.

Drew: You're a parent, and you find out your teenager either is doing drugs or has a gun. Which is worse?

Brad: What kind of drugs is junior taking?

Drew: You tell me.

Brad: Are we talking about getting high before
AP Bio? Or are we talking about shooting
crank while baby's getting breast-fed?

Liz: Is the kid doing drugs or on drugs?

Kevin: Is there a difference? This is still lit, but
you need to draw hard. It's a little clogged.

Liz: There's a huge difference. Is the kid a
recreational user or an addict?

Brad: Son, it's a no-brainer. I want my kid on
drugs. I don't care what kind.

Drew: Will you be my daddy?

Kevin: What if he says he's not going to use
the gun?

Brad: What do you think he's going to say?

Kevin: He wants to have it, just in case.

Brad: If he's not going to use it, then why have
it? By not having it, you've eliminated the
threat.

Jesse: Whoa! You can't make that leap.

Liz: Why not?

Jesse: Y'all are assuming a gun's a threat.

Brad: You're damn right I'm assuming a gun's
a threat! If my kid has a gun, he can use it,
and if he can use it, it's a threat to himself
and everyone else. He could cap me!

Jesse: Now, there's the discussion worth
   having!
Drew: Brad, what if your kid's a full-fledged
   addict? Or an out-of-control junkie? Better
   yet, what if he's dealing? Does that change
   the equation?
Brad: No. It's still a no-brainer. If it's drugs, I
   can relate. I'd be more equipped to handle
   the situation.
Kevin: Man, there's a huge difference between
   being a junkie or a dealer and doing what
   we do.
Brad: According to you, maybe. But a lot of
   people would argue: Either way, you're
   doing drugs. You're on drugs.
Kevin: And to those lesser enlightened I'd say,
   You have no idea what you're talking about.
   There's a huge difference between using
   and abusing. With a gun, you either have
   one or you don't. There's no gray area.
Jesse: Sure there is. Just 'cause you have a
   gun doesn't mean you're going to use it.
Brad: We're right back to where we were thirty
   seconds ago. Then, why have one, Jess?
Jesse: Y'all are missing something. What we're

talking about here is a regional issue.

Kevin: Regional? Man, what are you talking about?

Jesse: It's regional. The view in the Bradmobile isn't the prevailing view in different parts of the country. Not even close.

Drew: It should be.

Jesse: That's a value judgment.

Drew: No, to quote Brad, that's a no-brainer.

Jesse: Y'all need to hear me out on this one. You know how there are some issues where, no matter what, people can't see eye to eye?

Kevin: Like the whole red state–blue state thing.

Jesse: Exactly. Abortion. Gay marriage. Those issues. Both sides have firm beliefs, and one side can't even process how the other side sees things. That's exactly what this is.

Brad: My friend lives in the city, and whenever he goes clubbing, he only goes on gay nights.

Jesse: Jeez, Brad. Where did that friggin' come from?

Brad: I know I'm baked, but there's a chance

this may actually make sense. He only
goes clubbing on gay nights.

Drew: I get what Brad's saying. I've only been
clubbing a few times, and I've preferred the
gay nights also.

Jesse: That's 'cause you like it when the boys
make a play for you.

Drew: Well, yeah, it is flattering. It's great for
the ego when a gay guy thinks you're hot.

Jesse: I'll pass on that ego boost.

Drew: When another guy is checking you out,
you know you have something.

Brad: Can I continue here?

Drew: I have a good body.

Kevin: Here we go!

Drew: I work hard to keep in shape. I want to
look good without a shirt. And I know I do.
I have no problem saying that.

Jesse: If I didn't know better, I'd say you were
friggin' manorexic.

Drew: Watch the lot, tool.

Brad: Stop. Everyone. We're not talking about
Drew's body-image issues.

Drew: I don't have body-image issues. All I
know—

Brad: Enough! I'm making a point.

Kevin: Then, make it.

Brad: I will, but someone first needs to tell me what I was saying.

Jesse: You're a friggin' mess.

Brad: I got it! Gay nights. Clubbing. See, the short-term memory isn't all gone.

Jesse: It's getting close.

Brad: At many clubs, gay nights are the only times they don't have metal detectors or do full-body searches.

Liz: We don't get searched at the Creek.

Drew: The Creek's not a nightclub, but I have news for you, give it time. That day's not far off.

Kevin: There's an optimistic outlook.

Brad: They don't worry about weapons on gay nights.

Liz: Only people dying of overdoses.

Brad: That's every night. My point is, even nightclubs are more concerned about weapons than drugs. Weapons are a much greater threat and risk.

Drew: Nicely done, Brad. That just might make sense . . . although I can't be certain until I sober up.

Kevin: Hey, I'm roasted, toasted, and Kentucky fried, and I'm saying it makes sense. Way to go, man. That's the reason we don't have metal detectors at the Creek. Zig's never had to deal with weapons.

Drew: That's about to change.

Liz: What do you mean?

Drew: I just think that's about to change. That's all.

Liz: You can't just make a statement like that and not offer up anything else.

Drew: Forget it.

Brad: I'm with Liz on this one. Start talking, Drew.

Drew: I said forget it.

Brad: And I said no. Start talking.

Drew: Fine. But I'm not naming names.

Kevin: Why not?

Drew: Because you don't want to know names. You don't want that knowledge.

Brad: What are you talking about, already?

Drew: I posed the hypothetical about guns for a reason. I wanted to know your thoughts in advance.

Brad: In advance of what?

Drew: In the near future, I can say with a
degree of certainty, this is something we'll
be hearing about with regards to the Creek.

Kevin: Then, I'm glad we're getting out when
we are.

Jesse: I hate those friggin' intruder drills they
make us do now. They freak me out.

Kevin: You and me both.

Liz: I feel bad for Zig if what you're saying is
true. So far he's only had to deal with
drugs and sex and alcohol.

Kevin: Hey, speaking of drugs and sex and
alcohol, what's this I'm hearing about
Casey walking at graduation?

Jesse: Is that true?

Brad: Drew? You're our resident expert in the
field. Care to comment?

Drew: I'll pass.

Brad: You know you're dying to espouse some
new theory.

Kevin: Shoot your load, man.

Drew: Casey hasn't said a word to me.

Brad: I'm calling bullshit.

Drew: Let me rephrase that. He says he *can't*

say a word to me.

Kevin: So that means you do have a theory.

Drew: Yes, I do.

Brad: We let you stay quiet on the guns and
weapons theory, but not this one.

Kevin: Theorize, *por favor*.

Drew: Casey cut a deal.

Kevin: After all this time? It's been months
since the ski trip.

Drew: Doesn't matter. With Zig, it's all about
information and intelligence gathering. You
know that by now. Somebody knew something about someone, and whenever that's
the case, there's always a deal to be made.
And Zig's always willing to cut one if the
info is good enough.

Jesse: How can Zig give Casey a free pass
and not everyone else?

Brad: Well, it's not like he has to worry about
Shane.

Kevin: Man, I'll never forgive his mom for
pulling him out of school like that.

Brad: The middle of senior year. Type crazy.

Kevin: She went religion on him. He always
talked about that. And then after what

211

Andre did to him, it was bound to happen.

Jesse: What about Dex?

Kevin: Now there's a kid who's fallen off the face of the earth.

Drew: You're telling me. Why do you think the baseball team sucked so bad this year? He didn't play.

Kevin: Wasn't he the one doing the sucking?

Brad: You said you don't know why he didn't play.

Drew: I don't know why. I don't know if Zig wouldn't let him or if it was his choice. I don't know how it went down.

Kevin: We only know who went down on whom.

Brad: You need to press Casey for some answers.

Drew: I'll see him at lunch. Let you know what I find out.

Brad: What's the latest on Nikki?

Liz: Have they spoken?

Drew: Casey and Nikki? Not a word.

Liz: Joanne even stays away from her now.

Brad: Everyone said our trip couldn't top last year's, but, dude, we blew them—

Kevin: Stoner Dude alert!

Liz: Stoner Dude alert!

Kevin: Stoner Dude is in the SUV. I repeat,
Stoner Dude is in the SUV.

Drew: What bizarre and random words of
wisdom will Brad's alter ego have in store
for us today?

Brad: Like whoa, dude. Today I have
superpowers! No, like, I have more than
superpowers. I have super aphrodisiacal
powers. Like, every girl I look at will
instantly crave me.

Liz: Allow me to debunk your delusion. This girl
has no such instant craving.

Brad: Like, whoa, dudette. That was radically
harsh.

Liz: Reality bites.

Brad: Like, what's with the pugilism? The
animus. The disdain. I feel such
combativeness.

Liz: Shut up! You can't feel shit!

Jesse: Jeez, Brad, did you smoke bud or
inhale a friggin' thesaurus?

Kevin: I didn't think it was possible, but you
sound even more Cheech and Chonged

213

than you usually do. Keep the barrage coming!

Brad: Whoa, now it's like I'm peering at the spectrum of paranoia. At one extreme resides Sir Drew, in the land of the cavalier and the careless. And there, far across the galaxy, is the Jesse-Jess, in the world of excess caution and overprotection.

Jesse: What are you babblin' about?

Liz: Do you even understand what you're saying?

Brad: Of course, dudette. And, like, the seat upon which you sit is the bridge that spans the heavens and connects the opposing universi.

Liz: Universi? Shut up, Brad!

Brad: Type vicious, dudette.

Kevin: He's making perfect sense to me. Hey, any chance you'll still be in Stoner Dude mode for Questions?

Brad: Like, when I'm Stoner Dude, I always win Questions.

Jesse: Guess what, Stoner Dude? Five-Minute Warning!

Brad: Already? No way, dude.

Jesse: Way, dude.

Drew: Our last Five-Minute Warning.

Kevin: Man, I'm getting all teary.

Liz: Therapy flew.

Jesse: Not for me, it didn't. Smoke up, y'all.
I'm starting my tidying and calling last
bowl.

Drew: That takes on a whole other meaning
today.

Liz: Who's our last Munchies?

Kevin:I got it. I'll make the run to the Creekery.

Liz: Whatever you do, Kev, no chocolate. I
can't be breaking out for prom pictures.

Kevin: Hey, if I'm Munchies, I make the call.
Deal with it.

Brad: Whoa, dudes, check this out.

Liz: I'm scared.

Brad: Snack foods—they all smell like stinky
feet. That's why they all end in *tos*. Only
they, like, can't spell them t-o-e-s because
even if you had epic munchies, you
wouldn't buy 'em. Doritos, Fritos, Cheetos.

Liz: I guess that makes you *Toast*-itos.

Brad: Whoa, like, once again. The animus. The
disdain. So unnecessari.

Liz: Stoner Dude, you definitely don't need to smoke any more . . . ever!

Jesse: Who's Water?

Liz: Stoner Dude, you want to be Water?

Kevin: You're trusting him with a task? In this state?

Brad: I'll be Water.

Kevin: I'm not so sure that's a good idea, man.

Brad: Son, I'm fine. I'm Water. Just give me a second.

Kevin: Is that Brad? You back from Stoner Dude land?

Brad: Yeah, he's back, and his mind's in overdrive! I'm Doing Pockets now with Jesse.

Drew: I'm not Doing Pockets till the last possible moment. Give me that light. I'm taking every last hit on this very last day.

Liz: Good to the last puff.

Drew: No doubt.

Kevin: I still can't wrap my head around the fact that after this morning, Therapy will be something we speak of only in the past tense.

Liz: This time next week so will prom.

Kevin: Wow, that's right. This time next week
  we'll be done with prom.

Jesse: And nursing some crazy friggin'
  hangovers.

Brad: Hangovers? Speak for yourself. This time
  next week I still won't have gone to bed.
  I'm planning an all-nighter and then some.

Jesse: Two-Minute Warning!

Drew: The final orders! We're ready, Jesse.

Jesse: Water—capped and tucked under the
  driver's seat.

Brad, Drew, Kevin, Liz: Check.

Jesse: Lighter—dropped into front passenger
  door cup holder.

Brad, Drew, Kevin, Liz: Check.

Jesse: Pipe—returned to cell phone case in
  the console.

Brad, Drew, Kevin, Liz: Check.

Jesse: Nicely done, people. And now the last
  Doing Pockets call.

Drew: Let's have it, Jess.

Jesse: All Therapeutians, make sure keys,
  money, gum, Altoids, cell phones, wallets,
  Visine, Chap Stick, and student IDs are
  accounted for and in their proper pockets.

Brad, Drew, Kevin, Liz: Check.

Jesse: Okay, let's go, you friggin' potheads.
    We're outta here. Now!

What Was Supposed to Be the End

OFF WENT THE SONY.

That was supposed to be it. An outstanding final Therapy session forever captured on audio. I would take it home, upload it to my Mac, edit it down, add some music, throw in some sound effects, provide some commentary, and make copies for each of my friends.

The end.

But that wasn't the end. All this is the end.

Instead, enter you. This is the director's cut, with all the additional, behind-the-scenes bonus footage and commentary.

We all headed back into school, and after our respective trips to our lockers, the bathroom, and the Creekery, we met up outside Hurley's room like we did every day.

I was the first one there, and as soon as I got there, I knew something wasn't right. Hurley was late, and not once the entire year was he not in his room well before the start of class.

But when the Therapeutians started showing up, I

didn't say I felt things were out of sync, for fear of sounding like Jesse. All I did was turn the Sony back on. I don't know why I did, but I felt like it was something I should do.

11:09 a.m.

Drew: Where's Hurley?

Kevin: Hey, maybe he won't show.

Brad: Son, that wouldn't be cool. He needs to be here for Questions today. End things on a high note.

Kevin: On a high note. Like we are.

Brad: Give me back that water. I got ill cotton mouth.

Kevin: Go easy, man. If you kill it now, we'll be dying in Hurley's.

Brad: Where do you think he is? He's always here by now.

Kevin: Maybe he canceled class. A gift to his students this last week of high school.

Brad: No, I want to play Questions. What have you got for us today, Munchies?

Kevin: Friday is candy day!

Liz: I'll kill you if there's chocolate in there. Where's Hurley?

Kevin: Welcome back, Liz.

Liz: Did you get chocolate?

Kevin: I would never do that to you, it's all
Gummi bears, Swedish fish, and jelly
beans.

Brad: I'm liking the selection.

Liz: And there'll be plenty because we know
Drew won't eat any of this.

Drew: You got that right. That's one hundred
percent pure high-fructose corn syrup you
got there. That's why the entire country is
obese.

Kevin: Here we go.

Drew: That's the shit that's in soft drinks. A
twelve-ounce can of Coke contains about
ten teaspoons of sugar. One small can.
Ten.

Brad: Mr. Manorexia speaks.

Drew: Think about that. Think about how much
soda the average person drinks each day.
Our bodies have no idea how to process
that much sugar.

Kevin: And today's buzzkilling health and
nutritional lesson has been brought to you
by . . .

Drew: All I know is I have a ripped eight-pack,
    while your gut and his gut are rolling off
    your belts months before you even start
    putting on your freshman fifteen.

Brad: Water me.

Liz: We're halfway through the bottle, and
    we're not even through the door.

Kevin: Hey, I need another sip, too. Don't cap
    that when you're done.

Jesse: Where's Hurley?

Liz: That appears to be the question of the
    morning.

Brad: Time check.

Jesse: Hurley's got two minutes, and then I'm
    friggin' outta here.

Brad: Two minutes? Hurley's got thirty
    seconds, and then I'm—

That's When It Happened

IT DIDN'T TAKE TWO MINUTES. Or thirty seconds.

Because that's when it happened. Out of nowhere.
You. Brushing by and entering Hurley's room without
breaking stride. We all froze. Brad literally stopped
midsentence.

I know you saw us as you were going in, but you

didn't even so much as glance our way. And at that moment I had my confirmation. You had seen us that day in the parking lot. This was exactly the same thing, only set in a different venue. Confirmation of the Incident took place right then and there, not twenty minutes later when you told me in your office.

And at that moment I knew something else. Things were about to take a turn toward the unpleasant. Because you're never inside a classroom, Zig. Everyone at the Creek knows that.

We all shuffled right in, and during those thirty-nine steps from the hall to my seat, all I kept thinking was, *This can't be good; this can't be good.* I may even have been saying the words out loud, but I can't be certain.

I sat down with a jolt. I say that because once I hit my last-row seat, I was jolted back to lucidity. I was suddenly sober and completely aware. Aware of every aspect of this extraordinary turn of events.

Unfortunately, my friends weren't appreciating the magnitude of the moment like I was, but looking at the Therapeutians, I could tell everyone's paranoia synapses were rapid-firing. Brad was chomping on his lip, Liz was gnawing on her cuticles, and Kevin was cracking and recracking his knuckles. But it was Jesse—the sober one—who was freaking the most: fidgeting, searching the room, clasping and unclasping his hands on the desk, even visibly trembling.

I didn't want to start bugging out as well, so I focused back on you, standing at the front of the class, silent and stoic. You had both hands on the desk as you scanned all the faces. Then you shut your eyes and exhaled that endless breath.

Remember that?

Well, that was my opening. That's when I took the tape recorder out of my pocket, placed it on my lap, and said a silent hope that my Energizers weren't betraying me.

They weren't.

11:13 a.m.

Zig: I've never had to deal with a situation
    remotely close to this.
(Pause.)
Even I don't know where to start this time. Trust
    me, I'm at a total loss with this one. But I
    feel I have to do things this way. I wouldn't
    ordinarily, but since we're in our last week
    here, I don't know what else to do.

(Pause.)

The rumors are already starting to fly, and I
     need them to stop. That's why I'm coming
     to you directly like this. I'm not at liberty to
     disclose much, and by coming to you in
     this manner, I know I'm revealing far more
     than I should, but I'm doing so for a
     reason. I'm asking for some compassion
     and decency. Show some graduating-
     senior maturity. Resist that temptation to
     gossip. Especially about something like
     this. When we're talking about a man's life
     and livelihood.

(Long pause.)

With that said, let me backtrack here. Let's go
     back to your senior ski trip for a moment.
     Now, I'm not going to rehash that nonsense
     with you. There's absolutely nothing to be
     gained from that, but what I want to say is
     this: When incidents like that take place, as
     a principal, I hold out hope that in the end
     some good's going to come of it. In spite of
     all the misery and anger and
     disappointment and everything else that
     goes along with it, I hold out hope that

224

somehow the end result turns out to be positive.

(Pause.)

As you're all aware, one of the main students involved in the ski trip disaster was Casey Gooden. Most of you know him. As a matter of fact, looking around this room, I would say all of you know Casey. Now all of you know me well enough to know that I never publicly share another student's business. It's inappropriate. But in this instance, right now, I'm breaking my own rule. I feel . . . I feel it's absolutely essential that all of you know the instrumental role Casey Gooden played in getting to the core of what we're confronted with right now.

(Long pause.)

I just need to come out and say this already.

Get it over with.

(Pause.)

Earlier this morning Mr. Hurley was arrested. He was arrested on various drug charges, including possession and intent to distribute. He was arrested along with a member of the student body . . .

Zig, Drew: Andy Addington.
(Long pause.)

Liz: How did you know that?
Drew: Shh.
Liz: How did you know?
Drew: Not now.
Liz: That's why the Creek's run dry, right?
Drew: Not now. Did he hear me?
Liz: I don't think so.
Drew: I can't believe this was going on right in
    front of us, and we didn't know.

Zig: In the past, I've had to deal with members
    of the Creek student body who were
    engaged in illicit activity involving drugs.
    But never have I had to deal with a
    member of my faculty. This is a first.
(Pause.)

Drew: He's working an angle.
Kevin: What do you mean?
Drew: That's why he brought up Casey. No
    way is he naming names without working
    an angle.

Liz: What angle?

Drew: Shh. That's what I want to know.

Zig: I never . . . I never envisioned a scenario where a member of my staff—a trusted teacher—would be facilitating the use of drugs here at the Creek.

(Pause.)

Trust me, this is a tragedy.

Jesse: I'll say it's a friggin' tragedy.

Drew: Whisper, tool.

Jesse: Where we gonna get bud?

Drew: Not now, Jesse.

Brad: Did you have any idea?

Drew: None.

Brad: Addy got from Hurley?

Kevin: This is crazy, man.

Liz: Casey didn't snitch, did he?

Drew: No way. Keep your voices down.

Jesse: What do you mean, "No way"?

Kevin: Hey, this is why Casey's walking at graduation.

Drew: He's not speaking to the class right now.

Liz: What do you mean?

Drew: He's speaking to us.

Zig: I see a lot of you talking among
yourselves. I understand your concern and
confusion. Trust me, it's shared. So I'd like
to talk about this. I'd like there to be a
frank and open discussion. Ask me
anything.
(Pause.)
Questions?

Brad: Oh, shit.
Kevin: Busted.
Drew: Chill.
Jesse: We're fucked.
Drew: Everyone be chill.
Kevin: He didn't even look our way.
Brad: He wants us squirming.
Jesse: He's succeeded.

Zig: Very well. Everyone in here is dismissed.
(Pause.)
Except for the five of you.

Drew: Don't panic.

Jesse: Too friggin' late.

Liz: I'm freaking. . . .

Drew: Chill.

Zig: I suggest the five of you keep your mouths
    shut back there!

(Long pause.)

Drew: Admit to nothing.

Liz: We are so fuckin' screwed.

Drew: Don't say anything. No one.

Zig: Not one of you has a single thing to say to
    me?

(Pause.)

    No one?

(Pause.)

Drew: I do.

Zig: Then start talking. Now. I want to know
    everything.

Drew: Can I speak to you privately?

Zig: Excuse me, Andrew?

Drew: I'd like to speak to you alone.

Zig: Why? So these four druggies can get their
    stories aligned? I don't think so.

229

Drew: That's not why.

Zig: Do you not comprehend what is
    happening here? Are you that high right
    now? We're a week away from prom and
    graduation, and I'm about to parade the
    parents of five of my best students into my
    office so that I can tell them their children
    won't be at either. Nor will their children be
    receiving their diplomas.

Drew: I understand. We . . . we all do. But . . .
    can I please speak with you privately?

(Pause.)

Zig: You have ten minutes. I will see you in my
    office in ten minutes. And as for the rest of
    you, get your asses down to guidance. If I
    so much as even think you've uttered a
    single syllable to anyone before I make it
    down there, trust me, I'll be on the phone
    with all of your fall schools before we leave
    today.

Ten Minutes

I WENT TO THE GYM locker room. I knew I could be
alone there, and I needed to be. I stood at the back
sinks splashing water on my face, with my thoughts

racing a mile a minute. To be honest, there were a few moments there when I didn't know if I'd be able to summon the nerve to head for your office.

But I knew I had to. If not for me, then for my friends.

On my way, I tried visualizing all the different scenarios. Like I do when I play baseball. But visualization isn't easy when you're bordering on a state of panic. And when you're on the verge of panic, you tend to miss things. Things get overlooked.

Like still-recording tape players in your pocket.

Zig, it wasn't my intent to record our conversation. Honest. Bugging the principal? You don't think I'm that crazy, do you? If you had busted me, you would've expelled me. Or done to me what you did to Andre.

Yes, Zig, I know what you did to Andre.

I realized the Sony was on the moment I set foot in your office, but by that point it was too late to do anything about it. You had greeted me at your door, shut it, and locked it.

11:36 a.m.

Zig: I'm glad you had the good sense to show
up.
Drew: You knew I would, sir.

Zig: You didn't have much choice in the matter.

Drew: No.

Zig: Have a seat. We have a lot of talking to do.

Drew: Yes, sir.

Zig: How stoned are you right now?

Drew: Excuse me?

Zig: Andrew, you don't want to be playing
    dumb with me with right now. It wouldn't
    be wise.

Drew: I smoked earlier, sir.

Zig: All of you?

Drew: All of who?

Zig: Andrew, I'm warning—

Drew: Jesse didn't. The rest of us did.

Zig: Now that wasn't so difficult, was it?

Drew: No, sir.

Zig: Andrew, I know all about Questions, this
    little game the five of you like to play.

Drew: Yes, sir.

Zig: All your little rules, the system you have in
    place, with warnings and lookouts. I've
    known about it for some time now. Are you
    aware of that?

Drew: No, sir.

Zig: Stop. Do us both a favor and stop with all

the "sir's." And spare me the one-word
answers as well.

Drew: I thought you might have had an idea
about what was going on.

Zig: And what makes you say that?

Drew: You saw us that day in the parking lot.

Zig: Of course I saw you. And smelled you and
heard you. I'm not a fucking idiot.

Drew: I don't think that at all. You know that.

Zig: The five of you are in a world of trouble,
Andrew.

Drew: I'm aware of that, sir.

Zig: But you're the one in a position to do
something about it.

Drew: I don't understand.

Zig: Yes, you do. You understand exactly what
I'm telling you.

Drew: I'm not—

Zig: Andrew, there are steps that you can take
to help remedy this situation, at least to an
extent.

Drew: What would you like from me?

Zig: I meant what I said back there. As of now
none of you are attending graduation. And
forget about the prom.

Drew: So what can I do? The Therapeutians
　　will—

Zig: Don't you *dare* use that term in this office!
　　I know that's what you call yourselves. And
　　I know you call what you do Therapy. I
　　don't find it the least bit amusing or cute.

Drew: I understand. I understand everything.

Zig: Oh, I don't think you do. Do not
　　underestimate my resolve here, Andrew. Do
　　not misjudge the gravity of this situation.

Drew: I do understand, Zig. I understand
　　Casey told you about Andy Addington.

Zig: Excuse me. Don't change the subject.

Drew: I'm not. I'm just showing you I
　　understand. He did, didn't he?

Zig: That's none of your concern right now.

Drew: And Addington gave up Hurley.

Zig: Andrew, I don't know what you're—

Drew: And since you now have the five of us,
　　you want to see if I know anything
　　worthwhile. Which you know I do.

Zig: I beg your pardon?

Drew: You want information, and you know I
　　have information. Lots of it. That's why
　　we're here right now.

Zig: So then show me your cards.

Drew: No problem. Provided I get some
    assurances.

Zig: Andrew, I don't like—

Drew: Zig, I'll give you everything you want
    and then some. So long as my friends and
    I go to prom and graduation.

Zig: I make no such promises.

Drew: Then we don't have a deal.

Zig: Young man, you are in no position to be
    proposing deals in the first place.

Drew: I think I am.

Zig: Excuse me?

Drew: Zig, let's stop tiptoeing around. Your
    door is locked. Enough with the bullshit
    dance. We both know what's going on
    here.

Zig: Andrew, you are so far out of line right
    now I can't begin to tell you.

Drew: Am I really? As much as you know
    about what goes on around here, there's a
    lot you don't know, Zig. I can give you
    some of that.

Zig: Some of that? Not interested. Give me
    something huge. Rock my world.

235

Drew: Zig, I know it's not enough for you to
    hear from just one voice. You want to know
    about what matters to everyone at the
    Creek. You want to know what every kid is
    thinking when it comes to the
    things that count. I have all that.
    Zig: So then, tell me. Rock my world.
Drew: First, I have to know you'll honor our
    bargain.
Zig: We don't have a bargain, young man.
Drew: I give you all this, and nothing happens
    to my friends. No matter what.
Zig: You're not listening to me, Andrew. I'm not
    making any such promise.
Drew: I don't think you have much choice.
Zig: Did you just give me an ultimatum? Who
    in the world—
Drew: Total immunity for my friends and me.
    Total immunity—
Zig: Who the hell do you think you are?
Drew: Zig, you have a crisis on your hands!
Zig: Excuse me?
Drew: You're about to have a crisis the likes of
    which the Creek has never seen before.
Zig: You're full of shit, Andrew. I don't believe

one word of what you're saying right now.
You're trying to save your ass, and you'll
stop at nothing. If such a crisis really
existed, you would have told me what it
was by now.

Drew: Zig, you're not in any position not to
believe me.

Zig: Who are you trying to kid? I know the type
of person you are. If such a crisis really
existed, you would have come to me
sooner. I know what the Creek means to
you.

Drew: Maybe so. And perhaps I should have.
But who says it's my responsibility? And
maybe I was going to, but I needed to wait
until I was absolutely certain.

Zig: So now you're telling me this might not
even exist?

Drew: It exists.

Zig: What makes you so sure I'm not dealing
with it already?

Drew: You're not.

Zig: What makes you so sure?

Drew: If you knew about it, you wouldn't be
dealing with it. You would've dealt with it.

Zig: I'm not buying this, Andrew.

Drew: Zig, you have a student here on the
    verge of going Columbine.

(Pause.)

Zig: And you're keeping information like this
    from me?

Drew: No, I'm letting you know about it right
    now.

Zig: No, you're bartering it. Selling it to me as if
    safety and well-being were commodities.
    How dare you!

Drew: I'm telling you now.

Zig: Only because you're painted into a corner.
    Who is it?

Drew: No.

Zig: You have information about a student who
    may be about to shoot up my school, and
    you're withholding it. You're playing games
    with lives!

Drew: For the past few months you've had a
    kid bringing a gun to school.

Zig: Who, Andrew? I demand to know. Now!

Drew: One of Andre's targets.

Zig: Well, Andre is no longer here, so that
    situation seems to have resolved itself.

Drew: You would think, but that's not the case. This kid got pushed too far, Zig, and this kid is going to snap. It's going to happen, and to borrow your words, trust me.

Zig: This is despicable, Andrew. Unconscionable.

Drew: It is what it is.

Zig: You know something, Andrew, you are right about something. Let's stop tiptoeing around here. Enough with this bullshit dance already, as you so eloquently put it. Fine. Total immunity for your friends. But not you. They can attend the prom and graduation. Your status is solely dependent upon the information you provide.

Drew: I can live with that.

Zig: No, let me backtrack. You don't go to the prom. No matter what. That's gone. Whether or not you get to attend graduation depends on what you tell me. So who is it?

Drew: Not now. You'll get everything all at once.

Zig: You are not setting one foot back—

Drew: Zig, I guarantee you, what I turn over to

you will exceed your expectations.

Zig: I'll be the judge of that.

Drew: But whatever I give to you, I also give to
my friends.

Zig: Absolutely not.

Drew: Zig, I'm going to be saying things about
my friends to you, and I'm not going to be
holding anything back. Anything. That's
violating trusts. They have to know exactly
what I tell you. These are my friends.

Zig: Then each and every parent must know
about this as well.

Drew: There's no need. If I'm the only one—

Zig: Now hold on just a minute, young man.

Drew: Zig, there's no need for that. Not at this
juncture. If you're not satisfied with what I
provide to you, then by all means, you
should drop that bomb on all of them. Even
if it's the night before graduation. But I
know that won't happen. You do too. I'm
not going to let you down. You know me.

Zig: That's where you're wrong, Andrew.
You've already let me down. Far more than
you could ever imagine. I don't know you. I
thought I did, but if what you're saying is

true, you've compromised this home. I will
never look at you the same way again.

Drew: But I'm helping you now. And I'm also
helping my friends.

Zig: Your parents need to know. They need to
be told why you are not going to the prom
and why you may not be permitted to attend
graduation.

Drew: What do they need to know?

Zig: That you were caught smoking marijuana
on school grounds a week before
graduation.

Drew: I can live with that, too.

Zig: You don't have a choice, young man.
Andrew, this is so disappointing to me. You
have no idea. You're completely missing
the big picture here.

Drew: I don't understand.

Zig: I know you don't. That's what I find so
deeply disturbing. So let me tell you
about something else I know you don't
understand. You have a drug problem,
Andrew. And so do these so-called friends
of yours. You might not think so, and it
might not be the type of problem you read

about in pamphlets or hear about on the
news, but make no mistake, you, my
friend, have the makings of a sizable
addiction.

Drew: I'll take that under advisement.

Zig: Oh, you'll do more than that, young man.
You're going to drug counseling this
summer. Consider it a mandatory
graduation gift, assuming you do
graduate next week. I'll make the
arrangements.

Drew: I really don't think that's necessary.

Zig: I know you don't. That's part of the
problem. But trust me, this is going to do
you good. Because right now, I have to tell
you, I'm more than a little bit fearful that
sometime in the not-so-distant future the
best and the brightest the Creek has to
offer are going to find themselves in a
world of trouble.

A Day in the Life of Our Senior Year

IT WASN'T SUPPOSED to be this way. This wasn't what
I had in mind.

I didn't go to my senior prom. Obviously. I did

this instead. Lived up to my end of the bargain.

But to be honest, Zig, I have to say, there was something incredibly fulfilling and cleansing about this. I wasn't expecting that. I didn't anticipate such a sense of closure and satisfaction.

This was therapeutic.

And I know why.

It felt good knowing I took this hit for my friends, knowing I was able to come through for them the way I did. I didn't like having to disappear off the face of the earth like this without giving them a decent explanation, but I understand why it had to be this way.

They still don't know what happened to me. I haven't returned any of their calls or texts or e-mails. When Kevin and Brad stopped by, and then when Liz popped over, my parents told them I couldn't see anyone. But once I'm able to talk with them, and certainly after they've listened up to this point, they'll have the whole story. They won't like some of it, and I know I'll have some deserved explaining to do, but they'll understand.

They're my friends.

By the way, it's Jordan. The freshman. He's the one you need to watch. He's always wearing that jacket for a reason. You may want to check the lining and inside pockets. He's going to do damage if you don't.

And also by the way, I'm not going to rehab or drug counseling or whatever it is you want me to attend. That would be going against everything I stand for. It would be going against everything the Therapeutians stanf for.

This is who we are. No apologies.

We weren't hurting anyone, Zig. We weren't even hurting ourselves. We knew what we were doing the entire time. Therapy wasn't about doing drugs, and anyone who thinks it was can't comprehend us. No, we couldn't have experienced all this without the cannabis, but that's not what Therapy was all about.

Therapy was high school in a nutshell. And high school was about learning the secrets of life, discovering our true identities, growing up, looking out for our friends, and trying not to get busted.

About the Author

Phil Bildner is the author of the Texas Bluebonnet Award–winning *Shoeless Joe & Black Betsy* and its companion, *The Shot Heard 'Round the World*, both illustrated by C. F. Payne; and *Twenty-One Elephants*, illustrated by LeUyen Pham. He lives in Brooklyn, New York.